The Lost Child's Quest *is a he[illegible] mystery novel. Its thrills are threaded with the myths and annals of ancient Britain, and its young protagonist, Tia, is admirable not only for her budding bravery, but also for being such a compassionate heroine. In fact, Haddell's entire novel thrums with kindness and empathy, and that's a wonderful thing.*

Darren Simpson, author of *Scavengers*,
a *Guardian* Book of the Year 2019

James Haddell

The Lost Child's Quest

JAMES HADDELL

Published by
Emira Press
www.emirapress.co.uk

ISBN 978 1 91422 200 9
e-ISBN 978 1 91422 201 6

First edition 2020

For my four heroes:
Rach, Lily, Tom and Benji

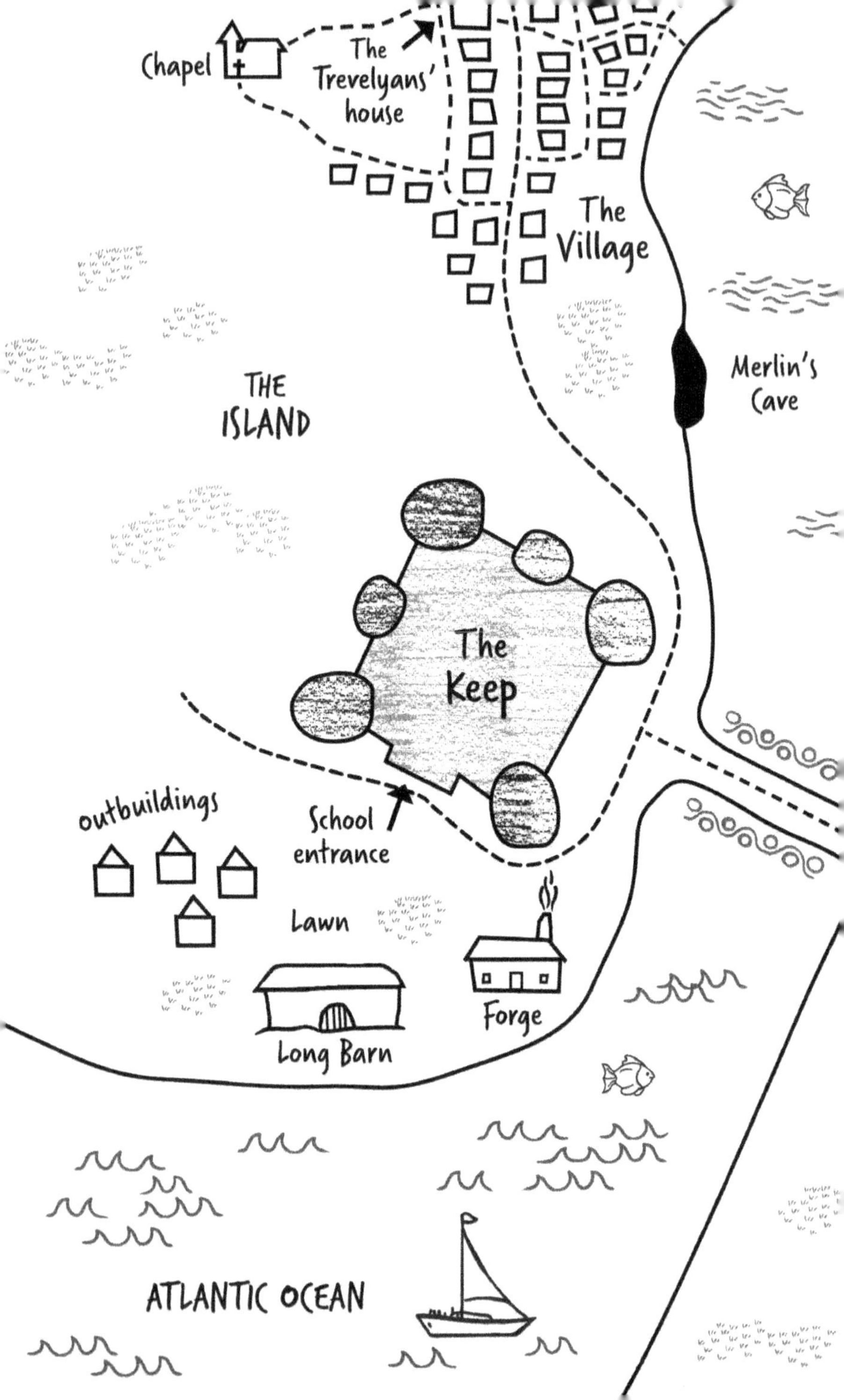
Chapel
The Trevelyans' house
The Village
Merlin's Cave
THE ISLAND
The Keep
School entrance
outbuildings
Lawn
Forge
Long Barn
ATLANTIC OCEAN

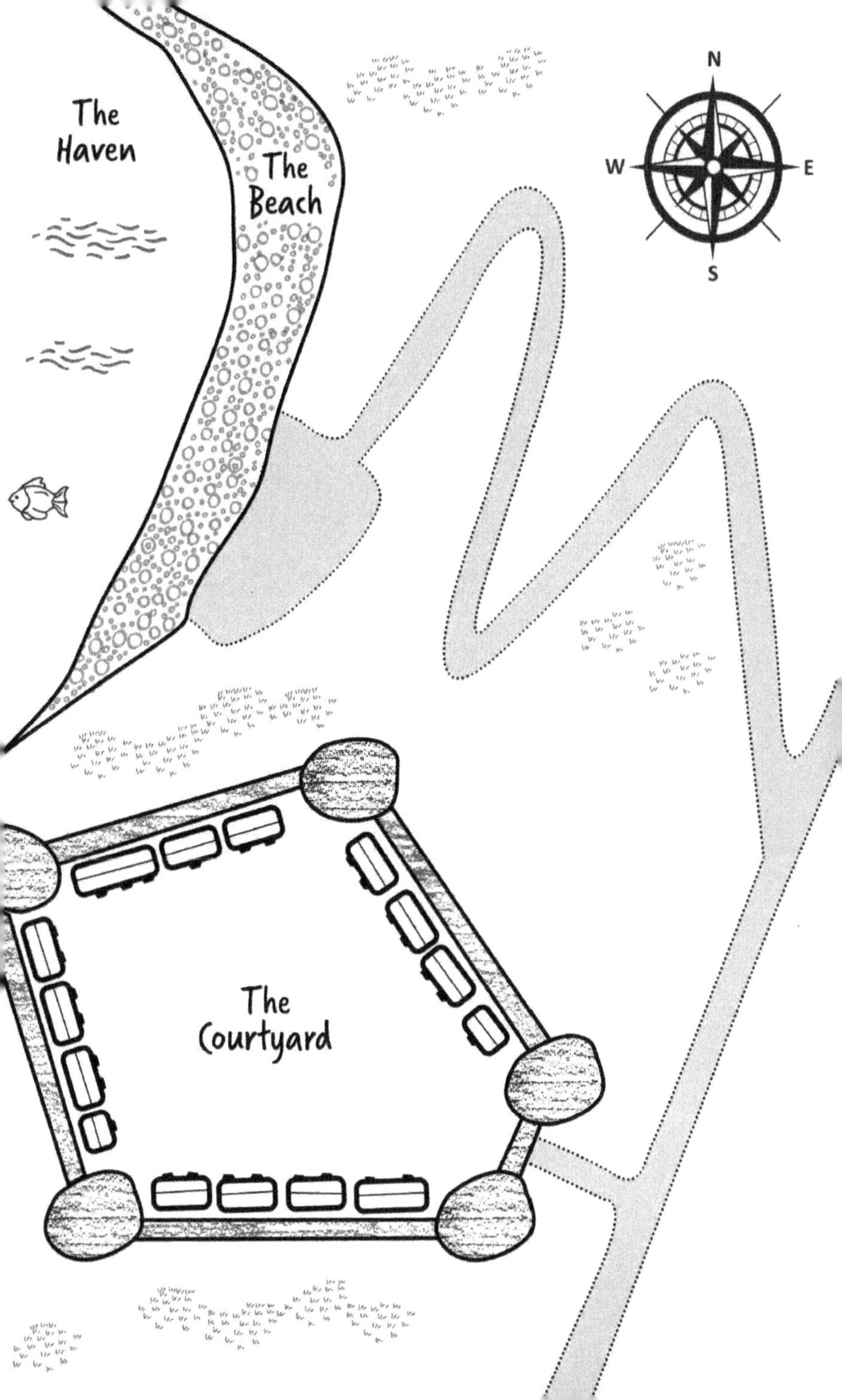
The Haven
The Beach
The Courtyard
N
W
E
S

Chapter One

Visitors

Some might say it was ironic that both the greatest threat and the safest haven Tia Hemyke had ever known were to enter her life within days of each other.

But perhaps it was fate.

Tia was almost ten, but she was smaller than the two eight-year-old girls, Kayla and Jade, with whom she shared a small bedroom. In fact, six-year-old Mary was the only one of the twelve girls living in Ms Davidson's house who was shorter. Tia had thick, dark red curls that bobbed across her shoulders whenever she moved. Her pale skin and large round eyes, the colour of a stormy sea, made her look as frightened as she often felt.

It was mid-morning during the summer holidays

and Tia was alone in the lounge of the children's home, kneeling on the sofa as she gazed out of the bay window. She was thinking of Mr and Mrs Trevelyan, who had visited her every day that week, and trying to imagine calling them Mum and Dad.

At that very moment, however, another visitor was striding purposefully towards the house; a very different sort of visitor, who promised anything but security. Tia first saw the tall, lean stranger as he paused beside the front gate to brush something from the front of his pristine-looking black suit with a look of disgust before casually opening the gate. His eyes moved around quickly and coldly, taking in the house and garden as if to make a swift appraisal and deciding the building wasn't the least bit important to him.

He knocked at the door, and Tia heard Ms Davidson shuffling out of her office and across the hallway to answer it. The door to the lounge was slightly ajar, so she could hear but not see the interaction that followed in the hallway.

"Good morning, madam. I wonder if you might be able to help me." The man's voice slithered smoothly into the hallway and through the crack of the door.

"And how might I help you, sir?" chirped the short, round lady.

"Well, for several months now I've been trying to track down a girl who was orphaned about nine years ago. Her father was a very dear friend of mine, though we lost touch over the years. We both travelled a lot, you see. I was devastated when I heard of his tragic death, and I had no idea until earlier this year that he had a daughter. Ever since then I've been trying to find her, and I believe I may finally be standing on her doorstep."

"My goodness!" Ms Davidson exclaimed in a shrill voice. "Do you know the girl's name?"

"My friend's name was Hemyke. Do you have any girls here with that surname?"

Tia felt as though the air in her lungs had turned to ice. Her breath caught painfully in her throat, and the lounge seemed to swirl around her.

Some of the girls knew exactly how they had ended up in a children's home. Kayla had told Tia her mother was struggling to look after herself at the moment, but once her mum was back on track she would come to take Kayla home. Jade had been living with her grandparents because her mother had disappeared. Her father had never been around, and when her grandparents died she had been sent here. Though sad, these conversations always made Tia feel a little envious because she knew nothing of her history before her arrival at Ms Davidson's house as a baby.

As soon as Ms Davidson had busied the man into her office and shut the door, Tia slipped out into the hallway. In contrast to the warmth of the morning sun through the bay window of the lounge, the coolness of the tiles on her bare feet would have sent shivers down her spine if she hadn't already been trembling. Tia crouched down and pressed her ear against the wooden door of Ms Davidson's office. All she could hear was the thumping of her own heart at first, but then she tuned in to the voices in the room beyond.

"Do take a seat, Mister…?"

"Silverman."

"Mr Silverman." It sounded as though Ms Davidson was hurriedly trying to tidy her desk, which was usually hidden under a layer of jumbled documents. "Would you like a cup of tea? I've just made a fresh pot for myself and I can easily fetch another cup."

"No, thank you. Please continue with yours, though."

"It really is peculiar that you've turned up the very same week a lovely couple has applied to adopt little Tia. Just like buses, eh? You wait ages for one, then two come along at once!"

Ms Davidson seemed to think she'd made a hilarious joke here because she giggled rather loudly. The man gave a faint, hollow chuckle.

"To think that all these years have passed, and if you'd come just two days later, you'd have completely missed her. The lovely couple hope to have everything completed tomorrow so they can take her home the following day!"

Tia blinked as her mind spun a little. They would be coming to take her 'home' on Saturday. She hadn't quite comprehended that it was to happen so soon. She had a sudden urge to dig her heels into the ground and pause the passing of time until she could be sure it was what she really wanted.

"Is that so?" The man spoke slowly, as if a great many more thoughts were whirring around his head than he was prepared to voice. "As I said," he continued, "I lost touch with her father many years ago, but I'd be keen to know a bit more about the last few years of his life and the first months of Tia's. Do you know anything of the girl's history before she came to live here? Did she arrive with any possessions that might give us a clue as to her story?"

The way he said the words "girl" and "possessions" made it clear that the girl was much less interesting to him than the possessions. She reached for the precious pendant resting on a thin chain around her neck. Her fingers traced the two familiar grooves of the pointed ovals engraved in the shape of a cross.

"She did arrive with a few things," Ms Davidson answered merrily, evidently not at all suspicious. There was the clinking sound of a teacup being placed down on a saucer and then she continued. "The police tried to piece her story together but didn't get anywhere, so any information you have about her father would be most valuable. I found her right here on my doorstep one February evening after hearing a knock at the door. I didn't see another living soul out on the street, and the only clues we had to her identity were a brown luggage label with her name and date of birth on it, and a few knick-knacks in a little pouch. I think she must have lost most of them now, at least I haven't seen them in years. Apart from the pendant, that is. She never takes that off!"

Tia's hand tensed into a fist around the treasure that hung from her neck, her knuckles whitening against her already pale skin. She thought of the others in the small pouch hidden under her bed, none of which had been lost.

"*Pendant?*" It was clear from his slow pronunciation that Mr Silverman was smiling. "Can you describe it?"

"It's a simple little silver thing: round and thick, with a sort of cross on one side."

After a short pause, during which the only sound Tia could hear was her guardian slurping her tea, Mr Silverman asked another question: "Do you have a picture of the girl?"

"Oh yes, I have pictures of all my girls!"

From the sounds passing through the wooden door Tia guessed Ms Davidson had stood up and turned to rummage through the cupboards and drawers lining the wall behind her desk. After a short while she seemed to find what she was looking for.

"Here she is – pretty little girl," Ms Davidson said tenderly. "Small for her age, but she was such a tiny thing when she arrived she's done well to get to the size she is." There was another slurping sound.

"Thank you, Ms Davidson, you've been most helpful," said Mr Silverman.

"You're very wel–"

Ms Davidson didn't have a chance to finish her sentence. Tia heard a thud like a heavy sack of potatoes hitting the floor, and then the sound of footsteps growing rapidly louder. Before she could get to her feet the door to Ms Davidson's office opened.

Tia caught a glimpse of Ms Davidson's body sprawled out on the floor, one arm outstretched with a chubby finger still looped through the handle of her teacup. But then the doorframe was filled by the figure of Mr Silverman, who looked down at her with smiling, snake-like eyes that darted from her face to the pendant around her neck, then back to her face once again.

"Hello, Tia."

Chapter Two

Chased

The suited man reached his hand out towards Tia's neck, but before it got close enough to reveal whether he intended to strangle her or snatch the pendant, her jaws clenched around his fingers. She bit down as hard as she possibly could before Mr Silverman managed to wrench his hand free. Then Tia spun towards the front door, yanked on the handle and darted through the opening. She tried to slam it shut behind her, but Mr Silverman had the presence of mind to stop it with his foot, still clutching his stinging fingers.

Tia had no plan other than to run as fast as she could. She jumped over the low wall of the front garden, desperate to avoid fumbling with the gate. She chose a direction at random and sprinted off. She heard the squeak of the gate behind her. Mr Silverman obviously felt he didn't need to be in such a rush to catch her, and had elected to open the gate. An image flashed into Tia's mind of her pursuer walking briskly after her, still bearing that cool, serpentine smile.

She knew she had bitten him hard because she'd tasted blood, but it suddenly occurred to Tia that he had made no sound other than a sharp intake of breath. His coolness panicked her, yet the panic somehow seemed to clear her mind. She became aware that she was still barefoot and that running on the pavement was beginning to hurt. She needed to get onto softer ground to have any chance of getting away.

Ms Davidson's children's home was on the very edge of town, and Tia was now running beside an open field. As soon as she reached the wide wooden gate, she clambered up and jumped down onto the grass. But in the time it had taken her to climb up, Mr Silverman had closed the gap between them, and Tia felt his lunging fingertips brush the heel of her foot as she leapt down from the top of the gate. She wanted him to curse her or shout, or to indicate in some way that he was concerned she might get away, but her silent hunter still seemed eerily sure of his eventual triumph.

She glanced sideways at the woods that backed on to the house and briefly considered winding her way through the trees in an attempt to get back inside. But she was barefoot, and the house offered little safety with Ms Davidson lying there unconscious… or dead. Tia knew she couldn't just keep running, though. Her legs were so much shorter than those of the man behind her that she was sure to be caught eventually. She needed to use her size to her advantage.

As she ran toward the hedgerow on the opposite side of the field, Tia's eyes desperately scanned along its length for a gap large enough to squeeze through. She saw a decent-sized patch of light through a hole at the bottom of the bush in front of her and headed for it, then threw herself to the ground and began scrambling through. Although her chosen escape tunnel was just large enough, it was edged with bramble branches that scratched at her face, caught in her hair and tugged her clothes.

Tia's arms and head emerged on the other side. A recently ploughed field with waves of dusty soil rolled out in front of her like a sea of earth. She wriggled forward and jerked her knees in an attempt to free her shirt and escape the grip of the bramble thorns on her baggy trousers. Her torso was out and she managed to wrench one leg free. She heaved the other forward, but it seemed to be snagged on a strong thorn.

Then, to her horror, she realised the grip on the cuff of her trouser leg was no thorn, as it began pulling her backwards. She tried kicking back with the other foot, but that too became locked in an iron grip. Her hands scrambled for something to hang on to, but the field was made up of loose soil. She was soon sucked back into the hedgerow, helplessly clutching two handfuls of dusty earth.

Still the man made no sound other than a slight pant, as if this were all just a minor exertion for him. Tia continued to hold the earth in her outstretched hands as she was dragged backwards on her stomach. She was about to drop the dirt and grab the trunk of one of the hedge bushes when she was distracted by an odd thought. For the entire pursuit she had remained just as silent as Mr Silverman. She hadn't once screamed or shouted from the moment she had seen Ms Davidson lying on the floor right up until now, when the chase was over and her fate seemed sealed. The discovery of this latent courage was strangely calming, but she would need all the bravery she could muster to have any chance of escaping.

"Now then," Mr Silverman snarled through gritted teeth as Tia's head re-emerged on his side of the hedgerow.

He let go of her ankles, stepped forward, then reached down to take hold of her shoulder and flip her onto her back. But before he could get a decent grip on her shirt Tia flipped herself over, and, with her eyes and mouth clamped tightly shut, flung a handful of dusty soil up into the face of her adversary.

While he was bent over coughing and rubbing his

eyes with both hands, Tia scrambled onto her feet and shoved the other handful of dirt into his open mouth. She then turned and sprinted towards the small wood that backed on to Ms Davidson's house. Her plan was to get herself out of sight before Mr Silverman recovered his sight. She only had a few seconds to reach the cover of the trees.

It was far trickier running barefoot in the wooded area than it had been on the grassy field, but Tia only needed to get a little way in to hide behind a large tree. Once hidden, she chanced a glance around the thick trunk to see if she was still being chased. Mr Silverman was standing upright, wiping his face on the sleeve of his suit. He looked in the direction of the gate with the road behind it, then over at the woods where Tia was hiding. He seemed to make a choice and began running for the trees, though not directly towards her chosen trunk. Tia allowed herself a few heavy pants of relief to recover her breath. He had guessed the general direction of her flight but clearly hadn't seen her.

Mr Silverman paused at the edge of the trees to adjust his tie and brush some of the dirt from his sleeves before entering. "Come now, Tia. There's no need for all this fuss."

His tone was as smooth as ever, but the volume of his voice told Tia he had no idea there were only four or five trees between them. As he ventured further in, Tia edged around the trunk of her tree so she would not be seen, carefully inspecting the ground as she went so as not to snap a twig and give her position away.

"I don't want to hurt you," he said. "All I need is that little pendant. If you throw it down where I can see it you can just turn and run home. I'd have no reason to chase after you then."

Tia thought briefly about taking him up on this offer but decided she had no reason to trust him; in fact, she had every reason to *dis*trust him. Besides, she wasn't sure she would ever be able to part with one of her treasures, which were the only clues she had to who she really was.

Although he was coming closer, Tia was still sure he had no idea where she was. If he carried on creeping along in his current direction, however, he would walk right past her tree. She continued circling the thick trunk, scanning the ground as she went. Her eyes landed on a rock the size of a cricket ball, which lay next to her foot. She silently stooped to pick it up. It felt reassuring to have a cold, hard weapon in her hand.

Mr Silverman was level with her now. His feet stopped, and so did Tia's heart. She was just a couple of paces away from him.

"I could tell you all about your family, Tia. You know nothing of Geoffrey Hemyke, do you? You must be so *curious*."

With silent strength, Tia restrained the flood of emotions that drove her desire for self-knowledge; for answers to the questions that hovered over her past, and for solid information in place of the imagined explanations she had of the random items she had been left with on the doorstep. She clutched her pendant again and pictured the contents of the pouch under her mattress, but then stopped herself.

He's trying to distract you, hoping you might make some noise, she thought silently.

The man took two silent steps forward, and Tia took two silent steps around the tree. She had come full circle now. She was finally behind him and he was beginning to move away. For a second she was unsure. If her plan didn't work she would give her position away.

Just concentrate for a few more seconds, she told herself, trying to steady her racing heart.

Without making a sound, Tia took aim and launched her rock at the back of the man's head.

He fell to the ground, spread-eagled.

She waited a few seconds, but Mr Silverman didn't move.

"House! Phone! Police!" she panted aloud to herself.

Tia turned, then raced out of the wood and back over the field in the direction of the gate. She clambered over it and ran towards the house, refusing to slow down until she reached the still open front door. Just as she was about to leap into the hallway, the slim figure of Mrs Trevelyan emerged from inside the house. Tia was moving at such great speed she couldn't help colliding with her.

"Tia!" Mrs Trevelyan exclaimed, dropping to her knees to hold the frightened girl in her arms. "Tia, you're safe!"

Safe.

The word echoed in Tia's ears, and she finally knew, in that instant, what it meant. She buried her face in Mrs Trevelyan's neck and felt Mr Trevelyan place a protective arm across her back as he knelt down to embrace them both. And at last Tia felt safe enough to release a lifetime of uncried tears.

Chapter Three

A New Name

As Mr and Mrs Trevelyan's little purple car did its best to speed along the motorway, Tia gazed out of the window and wondered what the future might hold.

Mr Silverman must have regained consciousness, because he was nowhere to be found by the time the police had arrived. Tia had no desire to find out if he would come back for her, but she didn't really feel scared any more. Her escape from Mr Silverman had shown Tia how truly courageous she was, and this discovery had told her more about herself than any information about her past ever could have.

Still, Tia hoped she would never have to be that brave again. As she had run into the arms of her new parents that day – on the very same doorstep where she had been left all those years earlier – she had let go of her worries for a moment. Perhaps she didn't need to keep herself safe all on her own any longer… perhaps.

Mr and Mrs Trevelyan were in their early thirties, and both had deep brown eyes that glistened whenever they smiled. Mr Trevelyan had short, dark hair and Mrs Trevelyan a blonde bob. They both put just enough effort into their appearance so as not to look scruffy, but no more than that. Mrs Trevelyan wore no make-up and Mr Trevelyan's face was never completely clean-shaven. Their clothes were clean but not ironed.

I wonder if it will ever feel normal to call them Mum and Dad, thought Tia.

It had all been such a blur of words and faces the first time she met them, a week earlier and back before the terrible Mr Silverman incident. She remembered Mr Trevelyan saying, "We aren't perfect, but we'll do everything we can to make you happy and keep you safe."

That word again: *safe*.

It had been hard to concentrate on anything anyone said to her in the days that followed. Tia had been able to absorb just enough to understand that the couple couldn't take her to live with them straightaway as there were certain legal things that needed to be done. However, they had promised to visit her every day until they were able to take her to their home.

The long wait for the first promised visit had been the hardest. Tia hadn't even been sure she wanted them to come again at the time. She knew in some part of her brain that she had no reason to mistrust the Trevelyans, but her stomach told her she had no real reason to trust them either.

The couple had visited every day, just as they'd promised, and had spent a little longer with her each time. They had said it was a chance for her to get to know them, and that she could ask them anything she wanted. She had learned that they lived in a small house by the sea and had a daughter named Meghan, who was just a year older than Tia. Meghan had also lived in a children's home before being adopted by the Trevelyans.

"Where is your daughter now?" she had asked them the day before Mr Silverman showed up as they watched the fish swimming around the pond in Ms Davidson's back garden. "Have you left her on her own?"

"No, no," Mrs Trevelyan had answered with a broad smile. "She's staying with one of her friends in the village. We speak to her on the phone every morning and evening. She's having a great time, but she's very excited about the three of us coming home so she can meet you."

Tia switched her gaze back to her new parents sitting in the front of the car. She hadn't been apart from them since the terrible ordeal with Mr Silverman two days earlier. Once Ms Davidson had recovered from the effect of the sleeping drops the intruder had slipped into her tea and the police had gone, Tia's parents had been invited to stay in the guest bedroom. This seldom-used room on the attic floor of the children's home also contained a small bed for a child. So that very night Tia had packed up all her clothes and the treasure pouch that had lived under her mattress for so long into a small rucksack, and said goodbye to the two girls she had shared a room with for so many years.

The short walk up to the guest bedroom that night had seemed like a hundred-mile journey. Attending a court hearing to ratify the adoption had been momentous, as had finally saying goodbye to Ms Davidson and all the other girls, with little Mary sobbing all over Tia's T-shirt, but it was that first walk upstairs to the guest bedroom that had marked the beginning of her life as Tia Trevelyan.

Chapter Four

The Castle by the Sea

"Here we are," announced Mr Trevelyan later that afternoon, jolting Tia out of her daydream.

She straightened up and eagerly peered out of the window. They were passing through a tiny hamlet that consisted of a few scattered stone houses, an ancient-looking church and a pub. All Tia knew of her new home was that it was by the sea, but although there were gulls gliding through the cloud-spattered sky she couldn't see the ocean. Something else, however, and something Tia hadn't expected to see at all, was looming up in front of them.

An enormous stone wall at least as high as a three-storey house, and with a stone tower at each end twice as high as the wall itself, rose up before them as they left the hamlet. Two more towers were stationed roughly in the middle of the wall, one on each side of a huge archway big enough for two trucks to drive through side by side.

"Do you live in a castle?"

"Not exactly," her new mother answered. She turned around to look at Tia and winked.

Behind this huge wall, but some way back from it, Tia could see a gigantic stone building. Its numerous turrets were of different heights, all joined together in one enormous structure.

"The keep," Tia whispered to herself.

She had often sought refuge in books in Ms Davidson's lounge, and one of her favourites had been an encyclopaedia of European castles. It was full of colourful, labelled diagrams, making it a good one for times when she was too tired or unsettled to process full sentences.

Tia pressed her cheek against the window as they drove through the castle gateway to get a good view of the portcullis dangling above them. Once they were through the archway she saw that the wall continued round to form a complete enclosure, with a fifth tower opposite the two guarding the main entrance. This fifth tower had a smaller gateway at its base and behind it, rather than within the courtyard, stood the towering keep on the side of a large grassy hill. Beyond that Tia could see only sky, so she guessed the huge hill jutted straight up out of the sea.

It's a bit like a motte-and-bailey castle, Tia thought, *though they're usually made of wood rather than stone.*

Mr Trevelyan parked the car among a cluster of vehicles in the middle of the vast, enclosed courtyard. "We'll be walking from here," he said. "There are no roads on the island."

"Island?" Tia asked.

"Strictly speaking, it's a small peninsula," he explained, gesturing in the direction of the hill beneath the castle keep. "But everyone refers to it as the island."

Mr Trevelyan switched the engine off, and the two adults turned around to look at her.

"I'm sorry, Tia, we didn't really tell you much about your new home," said Mrs Trevelyan. "It seemed more important that we got to know each other first, and this is such a unique place we didn't quite know how to explain it without showing you."

"It's an incredible place, though!" Mr Trevelyan said.

He was grinning so widely as he spoke that Tia could see all of his teeth, and his eyes seemed to dance with excitement.

"A castle or fort has stood on this spot for more than two-and-a-half thousand years," he continued. "It's been redesigned, extended and rebuilt countless times, and has a million tales to tell. It's been home to warlords, kings, knights and sorcerers, but nowadays it's home to a community of archaeologists and historians who are trying to unlock the hidden secrets of its past."

Tia opened the car door, wide-eyed, and as she did so a waft of salty sea air cascaded over her. Her eyes were drawn to the sky by the sound of gulls. There were dozens of them, circling and swooping through the air and landing on the battlements. As her new parents unloaded their bags from the car, Tia turned slowly on the spot, surveying the castle courtyard. All around her were single-storey, whitewashed buildings of various shapes and sizes backing on to the ancient wall. They all had brown thatched roofs and their thick white walls were gently curved. The enormous stone towers stationed along the walls were also curved, so that Tia couldn't see a single hard edge anywhere.

She held Mrs Trevelyan's hand and allowed herself to be led across the courtyard towards the tower with the keep lying beyond it. As she walked, she looked to her left and her right, above her and behind her, lapping up the sights, sounds and smells of this wondrous place.

"The courtyard is where all the historians and archaeologists work," Mr Trevelyan explained, "although we spend a lot of time in the library when we're not out on archaeological digs around the country. These buildings mainly serve as offices, work rooms and storerooms."

There were a dozen or so men and women walking purposefully in and out of the buildings around the courtyard. Some were carrying books and others were holding mysterious-looking objects. One very short man with a large moustache and a tweed suit was struggling to carry an enormous battleaxe, while others were carrying ordinary shovels. Several waved to them from a distance and smiled knowingly at Tia.

Tia was grateful that nobody came over to chat. She wanted to concentrate on the place around her rather than worry about saying the right thing to complete strangers.

"Through here is the bridge to the keep and the island," Mrs Trevelyan said.

They passed beneath the small portcullis of the archway at the base of the tower, encountering momentary darkness before emerging on the other side into brilliant sunshine. After the courtyard, which had been dominated by strong stone walls and ancient man-made constructions, the view before them firmly reasserted Mother Nature's supremacy.

Tia hadn't realised how high up they were, nor how far out into the sea the peninsula jutted. The water was an icy blue, but the countless sprinklings of white foaming surf and the sound of crashing waves told her it was anything but still. The sea rose up and blended into a majestic sky; blue with white tufts of cloud to mirror the surf below. The island before them pierced the sea like a spearhead, as if it were the summit of a colossal underwater mountain. It was on the sloping green of this peak that the castle keep stood guard.

"Isn't it stunning?" Mrs Trevelyan whispered to Tia. "It stops me in my tracks every time I pass through the gateway."

The wind blew playfully, tossing Tia's thick, curly hair up and down as it whistled around her ears. The saltiness filled her nostrils, and seemed to unlock parts of her that had never felt free until now.

The flight of stone steps before them zigzagged down to a causeway, which led across to the island. Even from this distance Tia could tell the keep was enormous, probably constituting a greater quantity of stone than all the battlements and towers behind them, though somehow it was still dwarfed by the natural landscape around it.

The family descended the steps and started walking along the wide, cobblestone path that had been laid along the crest of the rocky causeway hundreds of years earlier to link the island to the mainland. The walk would have felt incredibly daring if it hadn't been for the walls as high as Tia's chest on either side of them, which were made from the same stone as the path. With this thick barrier to rest one hand on, and the other still holding that of her new mother, Tia felt only excitement and exhilaration.

Vertical cliffs stretched away to the left as far as she could see. The mainland to Tia's right sloped down to the sea more gradually. The headland seemed to be reaching out for the island, as if it wanted to create a second causeway a mile or so down the shore. The island seemed content with just the one bridge, so the curve of the mainland had to content itself with a sheltered bay of crystal-clear waters lapping at a sandy beach. On this bay-facing side of the island, huddled together like a flock of sheep on a hillside, was an assortment of little white houses with black slate roofs.

"Welcome to your new home, Tia," her father said, beaming at her. "Welcome to Stormhaven Castle!"

Chapter Five

Home

Tia had been gazing out of her new bedroom window for half an hour and was still unable to tear her eyes away from the view across the rooftops to the bay. The Trevelyan house was halfway up the steep hillside on the edge of the little village. The only building further up, behind the house, was a tiny chapel made of stone.

"It's a great view," Mr Trevelyan had told her, "but it's like scaling Everest when you're coming home from a day at the beach!"

Almost all the houses Tia had seen were whitewashed with black slate roofs. They varied a great deal in shape and size, though none were especially large. Her new home was a small mid-terrace, much like those on either side. To Tia, however, the Trevelyans' house seemed to glow with an energy the neighbouring houses did not have, the yellow flowers in a hanging basket beside the front door shimmering with a hint of gold despite sitting in late-afternoon shadow.

The rear garden was tiered due to the sloping hillside and was mostly devoted to growing vegetables. At the top of the garden was a wooden stile in a hedge, beyond which lay the little stone chapel and the untamed parts of the island.

Inside the house was a small living room at the front, and a compact kitchen with just enough room for a solid-looking oak table at the rear. Upstairs, her new parents' bedroom and a small bathroom occupied the rear of the house, while the room Tia was to share with her new sister was at the front.

"Your sister's going to spend one more night at her friend's house," explained Mrs Trevelyan as she unpacked Tia's clothes for her, "so you get to feel that this room is as much yours as hers. She'll be joining us for breakfast tomorrow, though."

Tia had grown so used to the idea of the three of them being together over the previous couple of days that she felt a little unsure about having a sister as well. She looked around the room. It was full of signs that another person slept there and quite an untidy one at that. The other bed was the same size as hers, but upright tree branches had been tied to each of the four corners and a thin green veil had been draped over the top, as if the bed belonged to a woodland princess. Tia thought she could see vivid purple sheets on the bed, but it was hard to tell exactly what lay beneath the jumble of books, maps, papers and pencils.

A guitar lay on the floor between the foot of the bed and a bookcase stuffed with many more volumes than it was designed to hold. Several books lay scattered around the guitar, as if they had recently popped off the crammed shelves. An anxious feeling that she was encroaching on someone else's personal space rose up within Tia.

"Believe it or not, Meghan actually tidied up for you a little," Mrs Trevelyan said with a smile. "Now the mess is only on *her* side of the room."

"Will she like me?" Tia asked with a frown.

Mrs Trevelyan placed the folded pair of jeans she was holding in the bottom drawer of the chest, slid it shut and sat down on the bed next to Tia, taking the small girl's hand in hers. "I'm sure you'll have your differences, but Meghan is very excited about having a sister. Sisters do fight – I certainly argued with my sister – but Meghan was actually the one who said she wanted a sibling before we looked into it."

"Really?" This was reassuring, and also reminded Tia of some other questions she had.

"Why did you choose me?"

"I have one sister, Kensa, who is two years older than

me," Mrs Trevelyan said after a thoughtful pause. "But when we were very young there were three of us. My little sister died when she was still a baby. I was only four years old at the time, so I don't remember her very well, but I recall how the loss affected my parents. They were immensely sad, but it also made them cherish us more. Every time they mentioned her it was as if the memory reminded them how much they loved all three of their girls. Her full name was Venetia, but they called her Tia for short. So when we saw your name on the list of children waiting to be adopted we knew you were the one."

Tia had never even known there was such a list. She wondered how many other people had read her name without giving her a second thought. The world was beginning to feel so much larger than she had ever appreciated before. Until today she had never left the town she had grown up in, and she wondered how many more places and people there must be out there that she had no knowledge of yet. She felt very small and, not for the first time, a little unsure about this new life that was beginning to unfold.

Her mother sniffed and blinked, which pushed a small tear from each of her brown eyes onto her cheeks. She shifted her position on the bed and half opened her mouth to say more, but stopped herself and just smiled. Tia smiled back; not just with her mouth, as she had become so good at doing over the years, but with her eyes as well. She said nothing in the hope that her new mother might go ahead and voice whatever it was she was thinking.

She did.

"We also recognised your surname. Eight years ago, an eminent historian by the name of Hemyke died in mysterious circumstances. There are some who think he had unearthed the secret of a long-lost medieval hoard of treasure and was murdered for it. Hemyke isn't a common name, and we thought it was possible that you might attract the attention of some dangerous people. So we thought it best to complete the adoption process as quickly as possible. I'm just sorry we weren't able to do it more quickly and spare you that terrible ordeal you went through two days ago."

"The man who chased me, Mr Silverman, said he could tell me about my father," Tia said softly. "He told me his name was Geoffrey Hemyke."

"I'm afraid he may just have been trying to trick you," Mrs Trevelyan said gently. "Professor Geoffrey Hemyke *is* the historian I was talking about, and he may well be involved in your story in some way, but he was in his eighties when he died, so it's extremely unlikely he was your birth father."

Tia distrusted every word that had slithered from Mr Silverman's lips. She had spent so many hours dreaming about her birth parents, and the name Geoffrey Hemyke had lingered like a whispering ghost. It was something of a relief that Mr Silverman hadn't been a close friend of her birth father.

"Did that awful man say anything else?" Mrs Trevelyan asked.

"He wanted my pendant." Tia showed her the plain-looking treasure. "It was with me when Ms Davidson found me on the doorstep."

Tia stopped herself from telling her new mother about the other things that had been left with her, which she had safely hidden in their pouch under her new mattress. She had a deep longing to entrust herself to her new family, but it almost felt as though there were a small, dark creature deep inside her chest, screaming at her not to trust anyone. It was as though all the strings of her heart were pulled tight, and the tension this created in her chest meant she could only take shallow breaths.

After another pause, Mrs Trevelyan spoke again: "We would dearly love to help you find out anything we possibly can about your history, but you don't have to deal with any of that until you're ready. Maybe you should spend some time enjoying the present and dreaming about the future before we try to decipher the past."

"I'd like that." It felt as though her words were radiating from the bottom of her heart straight through her chest rather than coming out of her mouth.

Mrs Trevelyan grinned, then picked some fluff off her

skirt. "If it's okay with you," she said, "your grandfather would like to come over tonight to say hello."

Tia was excited at the prospect of meeting another member of her new family so soon after arriving, but this emotion was also laced with anxiety. When the doorbell rang, Mrs Trevelyan opened it while Tia looked on from halfway up the stairs. The wonderful smell of fresh fish and chips flooded into the hallway.

"Dad!" exclaimed Mrs Trevelyan as she stood on tiptoes to wrap her arms around the shoulders of the towering, broad-chested man and plant a kiss on his whiskery face. He lifted her off the floor in a one-armed embrace, the other arm clutching a large, greasy-looking package.

"Gwen, my girl!" he chuckled, gently placing her back down. He had the look of someone who had enjoyed every minute of his long life and had no intention of slowing down.

Mrs Trevelyan turned around, grinning. "Tia, this is your Grandpa Locryn." Although his face was much more worn, whiskery and wrinkly, they looked very alike. Father and daughter stood for a moment in the hallway, beaming at Tia with the exact same smile.

"I'm so pleased to meet you, Tia," Grandpa Locryn

said warmly, kneeling down and resting an enormous hand on Tia's shoulder.

Any anxiety Tia had been feeling was soon forgotten, and the rest of the evening passed blissfully. The four of them sat around the kitchen table eating fish and chips and talking about the family. Tia said very little but listened to everything that was said avidly, wanting to learn as much as she could about her new relatives.

There was Grandpa Locryn's big brother – whom Tia pictured as an actual giant – Great-Uncle Enyon. He was the captain of an ocean liner and would send postcards every time he arrived in a new city.

She discovered that Mr Trevelyan had three older brothers: Uncle James, who lived in Cairo and was busy excavating ancient Egyptian tombs; Uncle George, who was trekking through the Peruvian Andes in search of lost Inca cities; and Uncle John, who lived on a boat in the Norwegian Fjords and spent his time scuba diving to explore Viking shipwrecks.

Tia lost count of how many cousins and second cousins she had on her father's side, but it seemed as though everyone was involved in something adventurous or mysterious. Even her mother's sister, Aunt Kensa, an accountant in London, was married to Uncle Ernie, who worked at the Tower of London guarding the Crown Jewels or something like that.

"And how is your mother doing, Tom?" Grandpa

Locryn asked as Mr Trevelyan handed him a drink after dinner.

"I received a very excited letter from her a couple of weeks ago," Tia's father replied, taking his seat at the table. "She thinks she's discovered the wreck of one of Black Bart's pirate ships. I'm not sure how much longer she can keep sailing around the Caribbean looking for pirate treasure. She'll be seventy this year, for goodness' sake! She said she was about to lead a diving trip to explore the wreck. That might take two months, depending on the weather, so we may not hear from her again until she arrives for her birthday."

Mr Trevelyan turned to Tia. "Your Nana Ollie has the same birthday as you, Tia. She's exactly sixty years your senior. When we told her your birthday was the 5th of November, she said she would rearrange her entire autumn diving schedule so she could be here for it!"

Tia wasn't sure why, but sharing a birthday with her new grandmother made her feel as if she had known and loved this adventurous old woman her entire life. Indeed, by the end of the evening she had almost forgotten that this was the first time she had heard any mention of these people, or that the faces she saw in her mind's eye were not necessarily true likenesses.

That night, Tia slipped a hand under her mattress to check that her treasure pouch was still there before climbing happily into bed. As she lay there with the smell of fish and chips lingering in her nostrils, Tia recounted the names of all her new family members. Before she got to the cousins on her father's side she had drifted into the most peaceful sleep she had ever known.

Chapter Six

The Sister

Tia opened her bleary eyes to see a grinning, freckly, bespectacled face, framed with wild dark hair that was held back with a purple headscarf. The face was staring down at her, almost nose to nose.

"You're awake!" said the face.

"Aargh!" shouted Tia, jerking her head away and bashing it against the wall.

"I'm Meghan, your big sister. I just got home and crept up here to see you. I've been watching you for twenty minutes."

Meghan didn't seem to think this was a strange thing to do at all.

"I hope you slept well, because I've got a big day

planned for us," she continued merrily. "We'll probably be going to chapel first thing after breakfast, but then I'm taking you to the top of the hill before lunch. You can see for miles from up there. Bran says he can see Wales on a clear day, but I'm sure he's making that up. Bran's my best friend, but he's always inventing stories to show off. Oh, I should take you to meet him, too." She paused briefly and frowned, evidently thinking about when would be best to fit this visit into the day. "And then we'll go down to the bay and have swimming races, and I'll show you Merlin's Cave. It's brilliant in there, but a bit dangerous. If you're still there when the tide comes in, you're stuck! Apparently, there's a whole network of caves under the island, though, so if you do get stuck, you should probably just go further in and see if you come out somewhere on the other side! Anyway, I'll ask Dad if we can go a little way in just to show you. Actually, I should probably tell Mum and Dad I'm back."

With that she hopped off the bed, grinned at Tia once more – not that she had really stopped grinning throughout her monologue – and strode out through the bedroom door.

Tia rubbed the back of her head and wondered whether her new sister was just a little eccentric or actually insane.

"Hi Dad, I'm back… Yeah, Bran's got a new bike and we spent the whole week riding around the island.

I think I know every single track now… Yeah, we found that one… That one, too… It's not *that* close to the edge of the cliff, Mum."

Her parents were obviously playing a small part in the conversation, but it was only Meghan's voice that carried along the hallway from the kitchen, up the stairs and into the bedroom.

"His dad took us to explore the woods on the mainland on one of the days… Yeah, it was called something like that. There was a river running through it, and we had to cycle along the banks to find a place that was shallow enough for us to cross. It's called 'fording', and medieval armies had to do it all the time… Yes, I was very polite and said please and thank you. And I wiped my nose on the tablecloth instead of my sleeve… I'm joking, Mum, don't worry! I didn't use the tablecloth – I used the curtain!"

Tia got dressed and crept down the stairs, peering over the banister as she went. Meghan was standing on a chair to give Mr Trevelyan a demonstration of the subtle ways in which fording a woodland stream on horseback in medieval armour would have been different from doing so on a mountain bike. Tia didn't see why she particularly needed to be standing on a chair to demonstrate this.

"Why don't you go and see if Tia's awake yet?" said her mother as she slid a tray of potatoes into the oven for roasting.

"Yeah, she is. I've just been up there telling her all the things we're going to do today. She's so excited!"

"Meghan, sweetie, remember that it's her first day. Let's not overdo it."

"But school starts on Wednesday, Mum. We've only got three days of the summer holiday left and we've got to make the most of them. I'm just trying to help her settle in."

"Let's just see what she wants to do, okay?"

Meghan got down from the chair looking a little disappointed. "Okay."

Tia joined her family in the kitchen and, after telling her parents that yes, she had slept well, and telling her sister that yes, she was very excited about all the things she had planned for today, sat down to eat some toast and marmalade.

"We normally go to the chapel on Sunday mornings, Tia," said Mrs Trevelyan, "but if you don't want to that's fine. One of the reasons Grandpa came round last night was that he thought you might not feel like meeting lots of new people at church today. There's absolutely no pressure."

"Will he be there?" Tia asked. She had loved every minute with her grandfather the previous night, and the prospect of seeing him again so soon was delicious.

"He has to be there," Meghan exclaimed. "He's the vicar!"

Tia had been to church several times while living at Ms Davidson's house and simply could not imagine Grandpa Locryn as the serious man who stood at the front wearing funny robes and talking at people. She had never especially disliked the church services she had been to in the past, and the girls had never been forced to go, but it had certainly never been an exciting or interesting experience. Her new grandpa was possibly the most exciting and interesting person she had ever met, however – though her new sister was another promising contender for that title – so she couldn't quite picture Grandpa Locryn running a church.

As Tia sat in the little chapel that morning, it soon became clear that this was going to be very different from her previous church experiences. The chapel felt like a beautiful elaborate home rather than a stuffy institutional building. Instead of depicting sombre scenes, the stained-glass windows were packed with swirling chunks of vibrant colour, as if they simply wanted to celebrate light and life, and they stretched right up to the rafters to let as much light in as possible.

The pews were all slightly different, but each was thick and roughly carved, so that anyone who sat in one was ever-conscious that these had once been towering, majestic trees. At the end of every pew was a huge bunch of wildflowers. Each was bursting with life and colour, and trails of ivy wound in and out of the wooden rafters above the congregation. There was no organ. Instead, the hymns were led by a woman with silvery hair flowing down to her waist, who played the guitar and sang with such an eerie tenderness that Tia got goosebumps.

"That's Elowen Tresco," whispered Meghan. "I'm having lessons with her. She's amazing. A bit loopy, but amazing!"

It was a little strange for Tia to see her grandfather dressed in the funny robes, but this was the only similarity he bore to the other priest Tia had encountered. At one point in the service, without any warning, he ducked down beneath the lectern in the pulpit. Two hand puppets popped up and had a discussion in squeaky voices about how they didn't feel very special most of the time. When Grandpa Locryn reappeared, he stepped down and wandered up and down the aisle, recounting the story of how Jesus recruited people who would have been nobodies in their society to become his first disciples. He spoke with such energy and eloquence that Tia was captivated. She almost felt as though she were sitting on the shores of Lake Galilee herself.

The congregation seemed in no rush to leave when the service finished. Tea and cake were on offer at the back of the chapel, and people lingered and chatted for some time. A few came to talk to the Trevelyans. A woman called Wyn, who had a worn, leathery face, hobbled over to them. She wore khaki trousers and a matching wide-brimmed hat, which, judging by the straw-like strands poking out at all angles from underneath, was holding down a bush of wiry grey hair. She smiled at Tia but spoke mostly to her new parents, simply saying, "Welcome to Stormhaven, Tia", in a gruff but friendly voice as she said goodbye to them.

Others also seemed keen to welcome Tia without making her feel like the focus of unwanted attention, but she was glad when they had all eventually gone and it was just her and her new family again. It felt as though she had met a lot of people, but Wyn and Elowen Tresco were the only names Tia could remember as she left.

Grandpa Locryn invited himself over for lunch, which Mrs Trevelyan seemed to be fully prepared for, and the five of them made their way across the churchyard towards the stile in the low hedgerow at the back of the Trevelyans' house.

"Mum, can I just take Tia up to the top of the hill and show her the view?" asked Meghan before they reached the hedge. "We'll only be half an hour."

Once Meghan had convinced her doubtful mother they could get up there and back in thirty minutes, and Tia had assured them that she really did want to go and see the view, the girls were given permission. Meghan's estimation proved a little optimistic, as it took them half an hour just to reach the summit, but Tia was in no doubt that the view had been well worth the climb.

As she stood facing the mainland, the island seemed

like a secret land guarded by the formidable castle fortifications on either side of the causeway, with the rest of the country stretching away to the horizon. The mainland looked so much paler and blurrier that it might as well have been a wholly different and less vivid world compared with the sparkling island on which she stood. From up here, Tia could see that the little village occupied only a tiny portion of the island. Looking down over the other sides of the hill, Tia could see how wild and untamed the island was, with long grasses and thick thorny bushes covering the upper slopes and small, hardy, windswept trees governing the lower slopes.

As they began their descent, Meghan continued telling Tia all the most useful information she could think of concerning life at Stormhaven. She told her about a huge man, Sloan Cadman, who everyone said was descended from sea giants and used to be a sea captain until he lost his leg to a shark and came to the village to open a chip shop. She told her about Mad Morag, an insane old woman who lived in a rundown cottage on the edge of the village furthest from the keep and always spoke in ancient riddles. Aside from these two, most of the adults in the village seemed to be historians and archaeologists working on the Stormhaven Project.

"Dougal Dinsmore is probably the most intelligent person in the country, so he's in charge of everything. Bran reckons he's descended from real dwarves. He's barely taller than me!"

"Does he have a big moustache?" Tia asked, thinking of the small man she had seen carrying an axe the day before.

"That's the one! He could be a dwarf, couldn't he?"

This brought Meghan on to some of the ancient legends surrounding Stormhaven: of pirates and smugglers whose treasures were lost within the labyrinth of caves under the hill; of the medieval dukes and duchesses who lived in the castle for centuries before that; of the dark ages, when various kings of Wessex battled one another and Stormhaven proved to be an impregnable fortress.

"Legend has it that King Arthur was born in the castle, and before that it was a Roman fort. And they reckon Celtic tribes inhabited the island for centuries before the Romans arrived."

Tia didn't quite know what to make of her sister. Meghan talked non-stop and Tia had to concentrate so hard on keeping up with all the things she had to say that she hadn't really had time to form an opinion about the girl herself. She was beginning to feel quite tired, and realised it was less to do with the walk and more a result of the conversation, although 'conversation' wasn't quite the right word, because that would imply *two* people talking, and Tia had said very little so far.

As they followed a winding path down the hillside, weaving in and out of gorse and bramble bushes, they passed an oddly shaped rock, which was about twice the height of Tia and stood in an upright position.

"That's an ancient standing stone, probably Neolithic."

Tia had no idea what that meant, but judging from her new sister's awe-struck expression and whispered voice it was a good thing.

"Come on," Meghan said. "Let's go and take a look."

It was essentially just a big old rock, but there was something about the bizarreness of it standing in a completely unnatural position that struck Tia, as if it were looking out to sea and waiting for an old friend to arrive. Someone must have put in a great deal of effort to get it into that position, but the complete absence of clues as to its purpose seemed to make the air around it tingle with mystery.

Tia ran her hand over the cold surface while Meghan continued to talk. She couldn't be sure, but she thought she felt a very slight, almost undetectable vibration, like the silent purr of a contented, sleepy kitten.

"Aren't these things amazing? There are loads of them all over the country. We've got eight of them on the island. There are lots of theories about what the ancient Britons used them for, but no one really knows for sure."

Tia used her foot to push aside a weed that was growing up from the base of the stone. As she did so, the lines on the cold surface behind the plant appeared to take on a very familiar shape. It was hard to tell from a standing position, so she lay down on her front to get a better look. It could have just been a coincidence – the lines could have just been the natural contours of the rock – but they looked remarkably like a very old and almost completely worn-down replica of a symbol she knew very well: two pointed ovals intertwined in the shape of an X.

She rubbed the thumb of one hand against the familiar cross on her pendant and reached out with the other. Perhaps it was the warmth of the earth just below the level of the symbol, but this part of the stone didn't seem cold at all. She traced the lines with her finger, still unsure whether the symbol was really there or not, then placed the palm of her hand over it.

There was a faint rumble, then the stone began to lean away from her.

Chapter Seven

Buried Treasure

It moved so slowly at first that Tia wasn't sure it was really happening, but then it gathered speed and fell, landing flat on the grass with a thud. The two girls stared at each other for a few seconds before Meghan put her hands on her hips and frowned at Tia.

"Tia! You can't just go around pushing ancient monuments over," she scolded. "That stone's been standing there for thousands of yeAAARRRGGHHH!"

Without so much as a warning rumble, the ground opened up and swallowed them, ancient monument and all.

For a full minute they could see nothing but clouds of dust and do nothing but cover their mouths and try not to inhale too much earth. Tia heard her sister before she saw her.

"Are you okay, Tia?" Meghan gasped between coughs. "Where are you?"

"Yeah, I'm all right. I'm right here."

As the dust began to settle, she was able to make out Meghan on the other side of the deep crater they now found themselves in. The stone, which had been between them when they fell, had carried on falling a little further, crashing through the level where they had come to rest, to lie still in its own crater within a crater. As a result, the girls were effectively standing on a thin ledge that ran around the wall of the pit. They edged their way round towards each other and met halfway.

"This is brilliant!" exclaimed Meghan, squeezing Tia's hand.

'Brilliant' was not the way Tia would have chosen to summarise the experience, and she didn't know whether to feel frustrated or encouraged that her sister clearly didn't think their current predicament was too serious.

Meghan wiped her glasses on the cleanest part of her T-shirt, replaced them and peered down to where the stone lay. "I think that's part of the cavern network. Look, the walls are rock down there, but it's all earth up here. It seems to be a tunnel leading off in two directions." She looked up at Tia, beaming. "Well done, sis!"

Tia felt a slight jolt of awkwardness at being referred to as 'sis' for the first time, but couldn't help but smile back in response to such praise. The girls looked up and began to think about how they might be able to get out.

"I reckon if you stand on my shoulders," Meghan said, "you could just about reach the top. Come on."

Tia climbed onto her sister's back and then, leaning against the earthy wall, worked her way up to a standing position on Meghan's shoulders. Her fingers searched for something to hang on to, found an exposed root, and gave it a tug to test its strength. At the same time, however, the ground beneath Meghan's feet gave way and she fell through to the tunnel below. The root Tia had hold of didn't snap but was pulled out of the soil by her weight, and she soon joined her sister on the cave floor.

Meghan had screamed as she hit the floor and was already in floods of tears by the time Tia dropped on top of her. "I think I've broken my legs!" she blubbed. "I can't walk!"

Tia felt a wave of panic rising up inside her, but then remembered how brave she knew she could be. Adrenaline cleared her mind, and she concentrated on what she could do to help her sister.

"Will you be all right if I go to fetch help?" Tia said.

Meghan's bottom lip quivered at the thought of being left alone down there, but she reluctantly nodded. Tia glanced in turn at the two possible routes available to her along the tunnel. There was a fair bit of light coming in through the hole the stone had made in the roof of the cavern, but unfortunately the tunnel appeared to lead into complete darkness in both directions.

"Which way do you think I should go? Can you tell which way is out towards the village and which goes deeper into the hill?" She was sure Meghan would know the answer to this. She had a feeling it would take more than plummeting through the ground twice to make her new sister lose her bearings.

"That way," Meghan nodded in reply. Being able to answer seemed to give her courage, and she stopped crying.

Tia smiled and was about to set off into the gloom when Meghan grabbed her wrist and pointed over at something in a corner of the cavern.

Tia squinted into the shadows, and as her eyes adjusted to the darkness a number of objects stacked against the tunnel wall came into focus. There were several boxes, a couple of barrels and various other smaller packages. Leaning against the boxes were a few ancient-looking pistols – the sort she could imagine pirates firing with from triple-masted galleons – and perched on top was a small wooden chest about the size of a shoebox.

Tia stood and walked slowly over to them. The wooden chest was perched at head height. She ran a hand over the curved lid, then lifted it a little to test whether it was locked. It wasn't. It was a little too high to see inside, so she shut the lid, carefully lowered the chest down and took it over to where Meghan was sitting. It was promisingly heavy.

She set it down and the two girls grinned at each other, their eyes gleaming with anticipation. They opened the stiff lid together and peered inside.

They had been expecting to see the blinding glare of shiny gold coins and glistening jewels, so when it turned out to be just as dark inside the chest as it was throughout the rest of the cave, they initially thought it was empty. Both girls exhaled, unaware that they had been holding their breath. Then they realised there was in fact something inside; something quite large.

Tia reached in with both hands and pulled out a strange-looking metal ornament. It was a dull, brownish colour. The figurine had the head and front legs of a goat, but the lower half of its body was a fishtail.

"Well, it's a little disappointing," said Meghan brightly. "I was hoping for pirate treasure or something. But it's still pretty amazing, I guess."

"It's bizarre," said Tia turning it around in her hands.

"Hey down there!" A boy's voice drifted down, echoing through the cavern.

The two girls squinted up into the daylight to see the dark silhouette of a boy who appeared to be about their age, with thick, curly hair and sticky-out ears. He was peering down at them over the edge of the crater.

"Bran!" exclaimed Meghan. "I was hoping we'd bump into you today. This is Tia, my new sister!"

"Hi Tia!"

"Hi." Tia thought it would be rude not to say hello, but she couldn't help but feel that there were more pressing things to be said right at that moment.

"Is that the standing stone that used to be up here?" Bran asked.

Again, Tia didn't think this was a terribly relevant question given that she and Meghan were stuck at the bottom of a big pit.

"Yeah, Tia pushed it over." Meghan noticed a blush on Tia's face in response to this comment, so she continued hurriedly. "But then it crashed through to this secret smugglers' tunnel. There's loads of stuff down here, even some old pistols."

"Wow! I'm coming down to have a look." Bran already had a leg over the edge of the pit and was just about to start lowering himself down when both girls shouted at him to stop.

"Bran, we're stuck down here," Meghan explained, speaking slowly in order to convey the seriousness of the situation. "We need you to go and get help!"

Bran seemed to think about this for a short while. "Okay, but I want you to promise I can have one of the smugglers' pistols afterwards."

Meghan's eyes narrowed. "Brandon Corentyn, I will *shoot* you with one of these smugglers' pistols if you don't go and get our parents *right now*!"

"Okay, okay, I'm going." Bran waved and added

brightly, "Bye Tia. It was nice to meet you."
And then he was gone.

Chapter Eight

The Penrose Family

Two days later, Tia stood staring at the pistols, boxes and barrels from the smugglers' tunnel laid out on a huge table in a workroom of the castle courtyard. She couldn't quite believe she had found anything so incredible and wondered at the stories of adventure on the high seas that must have been attached to these treasures.

More significantly, however, she wondered about the great standing stone. How on earth had it fallen over? She was convinced she hadn't pushed it over. That would have been impossible. Yet what other explanation was there?

"Dougal's been in touch with a few museums about the smugglers' hoard," said Mr Trevelyan, inspecting a pistol in his gloved hands. "There's a smugglers' museum on Bodmin Moor that it'll probably go to. What's really interesting, though, is that figurine." He put the pistol down and grinned at Tia while removing his gloves. "It's definitely Roman. Tressa, our Roman Britain expert, has seen loads of them before, but she's never seen one that big."

A young woman with a round face and short blonde curls bustled into the room and sat down at a computer.

"I really don't know what its purpose was, either," she said in a bubbly voice that made Tia think of a younger, less frazzled Ms Davidson. "The other intriguing thing is that it was with the rest of this stash. My husband, Alun, is a bit of an authority on the history of smuggling in this area, and he says that smugglers normally just dealt in silk, tea, tobacco and things like that. That's what was in the containers you found. No one's ever heard of smugglers trading in Roman antiques!"

Tressa and Mr Trevelyan were clearly very excited. Tia left the two adults discussing possible explanations for these mysteries and went out into the fresh mid-morning air to look for her sister.

Meghan's broken legs had turned out to be one sprained ankle and, given that she was still able to climb up onto stone walls and furniture to share dramatic accounts of the whole adventure with anyone who would listen, it didn't appear to be too badly injured. Telling the whole village about the incident was all well and good, but Tia felt increasingly uncomfortable every time her sister came to the part about "Tia pushing over the standing stone that had been there for thousands of years".

In fact, Meghan was recounting the discovery of the smugglers' chamber to a captive audience in the courtyard right at that moment. She had been hobbling around on crutches because of her sprained ankle, which made listening to one of her monologues quite dangerous as she couldn't help but wave crutch-wielding arms around as she spoke.

Meghan was talking to a woman with dark hair that was streaked with grey and tied back in a bun. Round glasses sat on the end of her nose, and next to her was a boy wearing an identical pair. Almost as small as Tia, he had mousy hair, and was holding the hands of two tiny girls, who looked exactly alike and were perfect miniature versions of their mother. The sight reminded Tia of a family of moles, looking a little dazed to be out in the daylight. They were standing beside an old brown transit van that looked as though it had been driven around the world three times on its way to Stormhaven. The back door of the van was open, and inside seemed to be all the family's worldly possessions.

"That's my sister," Meghan said, swinging an arm around to point in Tia's direction and causing the boy to pull one of his sisters out of harm's way as a crutch whistled through the air. "She's the one who pushed the ancient standing stone over."

Tia cringed as she walked over to the group. The woman smiled at her a little nervously, perhaps wondering whether this sister was as crazy as the one swinging the crutches about. Tia smiled back in what she hoped was a reassuring manner.

"This is Mrs Penrose. She's the new *librarian.*" Meghan said this word with awe, as if librarians guarded the greatest wonders of the world. "I haven't taken you to the library yet, have I? It's brilliant! It's on about five different floors of the keep, with loads of spiral staircases and connecting corridors."

Meghan hadn't been able to show Tia much at all in the two days that had passed since the events of Sunday. Their mother had suggested they take it easy, especially given Meghan's injury, but they had just about made it down to the beach on the Monday to look at Merlin's cave from a distance. The castle keep, however, remained a complete unknown to Tia.

"And this is Pasco." Meghan gestured towards the boy, who shuffled uncomfortably on the spot. "He's nine so he'll probably be in our class at school. And these are the twins. Er, sorry, what are their names again?"

"Ebrel and Emblyn," Mrs Penrose answered.

The twins smiled timidly and hid behind their brother.

At that moment, the diminutive Dougal Dinsmore came jogging across the courtyard towards them, his big moustache fluttering in the wind. "Endelyn, my dear. How wonderful to see you!"

"Dougal, how are you?" Mrs Penrose smiled at Professor Dinsmore much more naturally than she had at the girls.

The two embraced as if they were old friends, Dougal Dinsmore standing on tiptoes to do so.

"Splendid, absolutely splendid," Professor Dinsmore replied, beaming at her. "I am so delighted to be able to entrust our collection to such a knowledgeable curator as yourself. Now, you just wait there. A couple of chaps will be along with carts in a jiffy to help transport your things to the cottage. It's just the other side of the keep on the nearest side of the village."

"Thank you, Dougal," Mrs Penrose said, turning to face Meghan and Tia. "See you later, girls. It was lovely to meet a couple of Pasco's classmates. I hope you won't have any more perilous adventures!" She whitened a little, as if suddenly envisioning Meghan and Tia leading her son off on dangerous missions, but she regathered enough composure to flash them a forced smile.

"See you at school tomorrow, Pasco," grinned Meghan as she and Tia turned to leave.

Pasco whimpered something in reply.

School tomorrow. It seemed incredible to Tia, but with all the distractions of the last few days she hadn't given school much thought.

"Did you say Pasco will be in *our* class, Meghan? You're a year older than me, aren't you? Surely we'll be in different classes?"

"The school's really small, so each class is made up of two years, which means we'll be in the same class, with Mr Teague. I thought it was a bit weird at first. I'd been at a massive school in the city before I came to live with Mum and Dad, but it's actually really nice. You have the same teacher for two years, so you really get to know them. The first year you're one of the younger kids and the older ones look after you, then you get to look after a new batch of younger ones the year after."

Tia wasn't quite sure how she felt about being looked after by Meghan at school. She really liked her – it would have been impossible to go through the perils they had gone through on Sunday without warming to her – but she didn't want to be in her shadow the whole time at her new school. She toyed with the idea of asking Mrs Trevelyan to have a word with Meghan.

"Where is the school?" Tia had explored much of the village with Mr Trevelyan the day before, after a morning walk to the beach, but had seen nothing that looked like a school building.

"I'll show you on the way home."

It was strange enough that Meghan had answered in only seven words and turned down the chance to go off on another long monologue, but the way her eyes glinted mischievously made Tia's imagination race.

The sisters were meandering across the courtyard when Meghan stopped and, staring across at one of the corner towers, whispered, "Look!"

A big, shiny four-wheel-drive had just pulled into the courtyard and come to a stop in front of a door at the base of the tower. Out of the car stepped three middle-aged men in suits, one of whom opened the fourth door for an extremely elderly man to get out. He had white hair and a white beard, and he looked as though he might topple over if the wind blew too hard.

"Ah, Gwydre. Just driving through that gate makes me feel ten years younger," he said to one of the men who had offered him an arm to lean on.

"Well, Dad," Gwydre replied, "that still makes you pretty ancient, so don't you go running off around the battlements."

The old man gave a hearty if somewhat raspy laugh, and the two of them followed the other two men through the tower door.

"Hello, girls!" said a familiar voice from behind Tia and Meghan.

They turned to see Grandpa Locryn and their mother walking towards them. Their grandfather embraced them simultaneously in his huge arms.

"Do you know who those men are, Grandpa?" Meghan asked.

"That's Lord Reginald Thunderford and his two sons. I think the fourth fella must be the family lawyer. Lord Reg owns Stormhaven Castle and the island. He used to be around here loads – he's one of the keenest and most knowledgeable amateur historians you could ever meet – but he's getting on a bit now, and health problems have meant he's barely made it to the castle at all in the last few years."

"Wow!" Meghan exclaimed. "I never thought of anyone owning Stormhaven before. He must be so rich!"

"Yep. He's a wonderful man, though," Grandpa Locryn added.

"He's kept this community going for the last fifty years," said Mrs Trevelyan.

"That's right," said Grandpa Locryn, scratching his whiskery chin thoughtfully. "Though I'm not sure his sons will be so supportive once he's gone."

"I wonder why he's made the effort to come here today," Tia puzzled aloud.

"I'll come over and tell you later if you want."

The girls looked inquiringly at their grandfather.

"He's invited a few of us to a meeting," he continued, puffing out his chest a little, "which is why I'm here. I wasn't given any more information than that, but if their lawyer's here I reckon it must be something to do with making arrangements for this place once he's passed on."

"Afternoon, Locryn." Wyn limping over to join them. "How are you, Gwen? Hi, girls."

"Hello, Wyn. Have you been invited to the meeting too?" Grandpa Locryn enquired, shaking the woman by the hand.

"Yes," Wyn replied. "No idea what it's about. We'd better get moving, though. Dougal's going in already." She pointed a rough, stubby finger at tiny Professor Dinsmore, who was scurrying into the same tower Lord Reg had disappeared into before him.

"I'll come by and tell you all about it later," said Grandpa Locryn, ruffling the girls' hair and walking towards the tower door with Wyn.

"Come on, you two," said Mrs Trevelyan. "Time to get home for lunch."

They crossed the causeway, and as they approached the keep Tia reminded Meghan of her promise to point out the school.

"Follow me," Meghan said, hobbling around the opposite side of the keep to the way they would normally go to get home, while Mrs Trevelyan headed back to the house to get lunch ready.

A small stone staircase with about ten steps led up the side of the main building to a shorter tower that looked as though it was growing out of the side of the huge castle keep. In front of the tower was a large, well-kept lawn, around which sat a few small, round stone buildings and one long timber building, all with thatched roofs. Standing on the lawn, Meghan pointed back towards the tower and staircase with a crutch. Engraved in the stonework in large letters were the words:

Stormhaven Castle School of Exploration and Discovery

Chapter Nine

Thirteen Treasures

"The school is in the castle?!" Tia asked. "Is it a proper school?" Things weren't quite adding up in her mind. She pictured the type of relaxed, colourful education zone often found in museums but figured there must be another duller school with the usual tarmacked playground and classrooms with plastic furniture somewhere.

"A proper school? It's a *brilliant* school! The classrooms are the castle's old bedchambers. We eat lunch in the feasting hall, we explore the forests and map out the island, we research all sorts of historical periods in the library, we dress up in clothes from the olden days and learn how to make horseshoes in the iron forges. We even recreate battles dressed up in pretend armour and fight with foam weapons!"

It still didn't sound quite like a proper school to Tia, but it did sound brilliant.

They wandered home to find thick ham sandwiches waiting for them on the kitchen table, their mother already seated and reading an ancient-looking book while she ate. Over lunch, Meghan and Mrs Trevelyan explained a little more about the school and managed to convince Tia that it was indeed 'a proper school.'

"It's just that the headteacher, Ms Morgan, thinks children learn best when they're active," said Mrs Trevelyan, "and when they're immersed in an experience rather than sitting at a desk."

At this point, Meghan cut in with stories about Ms Morgan spending the summer holidays trekking through the Amazon rainforest in search of indigenous tribes as they hunted jungle animals with poison darts and blowpipes, and of riding bareback with nomads on the Tibetan Plateau.

"Last year she spent a month living with the Maasai people on the African plains and brought back a huge tribal shield. She had a spear, too, but it got confiscated at customs."

Meghan had raised one of her crutches like a javelin as she spoke, so Mrs Trevelyan gently took it off her and leaned it against the wall out of reach.

It all sounded so fantastic to Tia, but then every aspect

of her new life at Stormhaven seemed fantastic, like a completely different reality from the one she had grown up knowing. She was a little on edge most of the time, partly through excitement and partly through a fear of the unknown. It was a bit like being on a rollercoaster in the dark.

Meghan had a guitar lesson with Elowen Tresco that afternoon, which gave Tia a couple of hours alone with her mother. After washing up the lunch things, they settled themselves down in the sitting room, Mrs Trevelyan with a thick, dusty book and Tia with a book of tales about King Arthur and Merlin the wizard.

She had read it many times before, as Ms Davidson also had a copy. She had used books as a place of sanctuary back then – as a way to shut out the world and recover from the traumas of life. Now she was simply using books to give herself space to be calm and think. She didn't need the protection so much and felt able to put the book down every so often to ask her mother questions about school or some other aspect of Stormhaven life.

Reading how King Arthur had been born and then taken away by Merlin and entrusted into the care of Sir Ector for his own safety got Tia thinking about her own history and how much mystery still surrounded her past. She hadn't planned to take Mrs Trevelyan up on the offer of helping her search for answers just yet. Perhaps because she had been thinking about so many other things lately and hadn't worked up any anxiety over the subject, she felt a sense of calm at the idea of talking about her story with her new mother.

Without a word, Tia slipped up to her room and returned clutching a small leather pouch in her hand. "Can I show you something?" she said quietly.

"Of course," Mrs Trevelyan said softly, putting her book down on a side table. "What is it?"

"When I was left on the doorstep of Ms Davidson's house, a few things were left with me. There was a label that just had 'Tia Hemyke' and my birthday written on it, and a little bag with some things inside." Tia handed the pouch to her mother and undid the clasp at the back of her neck to take the pendant off. She held it thoughtfully in her hand. "I have no idea what any of them mean, but I've kept them like treasures my whole life."

Mrs Trevelyan gently emptied the contents of the little leather bag into her lap. Tia had barely removed the objects from their bag in the last couple of years, as she knew them so well she didn't need to, so it seemed strange to see them being handled by another person. They looked so familiar, yet slightly changed somehow. Or perhaps she was different rather than her treasures.

There they were: the twelve silvery, coin-shaped pieces of metal, four with a simple cross engraved on them and eight with a circle, and all of them a complete mystery to Tia.

Mrs Trevelyan picked each one up in turn and set them on top of the book she had been reading so as to see them more clearly. She handled them as carefully as Mr Trevelyan had examined the pistol earlier that morning. Each one seemed to be a wonder to her, and it meant a lot to Tia that they were being treated with such reverence.

"Twelve little treasures," she said at length, handing the empty pouch back to Tia.

"Thirteen," Tia corrected her, slipping the pouch into her pocket with one hand and opening the other to reveal the necklace she had been holding. "This was in there, too." She placed the pendant with the strange symbol on it alongside the other items on top of the book.

"*Thirteen* treasures," Mrs Trevelyan whispered to herself thoughtfully.

"The pendant's got this X-shaped symbol on one side, and I'm sure I saw the same symbol on the standing stone. That's why I touched it. But I didn't push it over, I'm sure I didn't!"

"Don't worry about that silly old stone now." Mrs Trevelyan took Tia's hand and squeezed it reassuringly. "Can I show these to your dad when he gets home? He might have some ideas."

Tia shifted a little awkwardly, as she did every time Mr or Mrs Trevelyan referred to themselves as Mum or Dad, but she agreed to the suggestion nonetheless.

Having carried the pendant like a weight around her neck for so many years, Tia had been unaware of the pressure it exerted on her. It was as if she hadn't realised how heavy the pendant was until she took it off and entrusted it into someone else's care. She had guarded the treasures so fiercely and for so long, but now that she had lain them down she felt no compulsion to take them up again anytime soon.

Tia was in her room when Mr Trevelyan came home, but she heard Mrs Trevelyan leading him straight into the living room to show him the thirteen items. By the time Tia had ventured downstairs, her new parents had finished discussing them and were coming to meet her in the hallway.

"Those are some very interesting little treasures you've got there, Tia," Mr Trevelyan said warmly. "Would you mind if I took them to work with me tomorrow to have a closer look at them? I can do a few tests that won't damage them at all but may tell us a bit more."

"No, that's fine," she answered. "Do you have any idea what they might mean?"

Mr Trevelyan gave his wife a look, as if he wasn't at all sure how much to say. Then he turned back to face Tia. "I'm sorry, Tia. We're not really sure."

"We're going to try to find out exactly what Geoffrey Hemyke was working on when he died," Mrs Trevelyan added. "That might give us a few more clues."

Tia felt certain they had some idea about their origin. Perhaps they were just reluctant to tell her until they had more solid evidence to back their ideas up, but she could sense something inside questioning why they would keep things from her if they were really to be trusted. She wondered whether to press them or not, but then there was a noise outside the door and the opportunity to do so had passed.

"Right," said Meghan, bursting through the door with her guitar case on her back and dragging Grandpa Locryn along behind her, which was quite a feat given that she was also carrying two crutches. "We're home and everyone's here! Now will you tell us what that meeting was all about, Grandpa?"

"You put the kettle on and I'll tell you all about it."

Chapter Ten

The Seven Stewards of Stormhaven

It seemed Grandpa Locryn had been correct; the meeting had indeed been set up to lay out the plans for Stormhaven's future.

"Lord Reg said he wants to set up a board of trustees to look after the place and ensure the community's long-term survival as a 'centre committed to the ongoing exploration and discovery of our nation's heritage'," he explained. "He invited all of us who were there to become founding members of the board. 'Stewards of Stormhaven' he called us. He likes things to sound grand!" Grandpa Locryn chuckled and took a slurp of tea.

"Who will the other stewards be?" asked Meghan. Tia could tell from the glint in her eyes that she also quite liked the grandeur of the title.

"Well, there was me, Dougal, Wyn, and then Lord Reg said he'd also spoken at length with your headteacher, Ms Morgan. She's accepted the position, sending her regrets that she hadn't arrived back in time for the meeting. Apparently, she had some trouble boarding her flight from Kyoto with her samurai sword."

Meghan grinned from ear to ear in response to this story and nodded at Tia, as if to say: "See, I told you she was amazing."

"It all got straightened out in the end, but she had to get a flight the next day," he added.

"Well, everything'll be fine if you four are in charge," concluded Meghan, leaning back in her chair as if there were nothing else in the world to worry about.

"We're also going to be joined by a lady from the family's law firm, who wasn't present either. She'd sent along a representative, the fourth chap who was in the car earlier. And Lord Reg's sons, Gwydre and Llacheu, will be the sixth and seventh members."

"What are their names again?" Meghan asked, her eyebrows raised as far as they could possibly go.

"They're very old Welsh names," Grandpa Locryn said, clearly amused at Meghan's reaction.

"Lord Reg is a bit of a King Arthur enthusiast,"

Mrs Trevelyan said. "Gwydre and Llacheu were two of Arthur's sons, according to some Welsh legends."

"It's a bit mean to give your children names like that, though," Meghan said, shaking her head in pity for the two men.

"How do his sons feel about the estate passing into the hands of a board of trustees rather than simply going to them?" Mr Trevelyan asked.

"It was a little difficult to tell," Grandpa Locryn replied thoughtfully. "Neither has ever taken much interest in the place, and Lord Reg has a great fortune aside from Stormhaven, so they've no real reason to complain. I don't think the youngest son Gwydre is too bothered, but Wyn heard that Llacheu has been trying to convince his father to turn the castle into a hotel for years."

Meghan gasped, as if this were utterly unthinkable.

"She reckons that's why Lord Reg came up with this trustees plan," he continued.

"Good thing, too! We can't let anyone turn Stormhaven into a *hotel*! You won't let him, will you, Grandpa?"

Mrs Trevelyan put a reassuring hand on her daughter's shoulder, as it looked as though Meghan was about to stand up on her chair in distress.

"Well, any future decisions will have to be agreed by at least four of the seven board members, so I don't fancy his chances." Grandpa Locryn gave Meghan a reassuring wink.

Conversation for the rest of the evening was focused on the first day of school. Mrs Trevelyan told Tia stories of when she had been at the school herself years before. She was just as enthusiastic as Meghan had been about the school, though perhaps not as energetic. Ms Morgan had also been the headteacher back then, and given all the interesting stories Tia had heard, the woman was quickly becoming something of a heroine in her mind.

"What's my teacher like?" Tia asked.

"Oh, Mr Teague is brilliant!" Tia had directed her question at the adults, but Meghan was never one to let an opportunity for getting excited about something pass her by. "He's really into historical battles. He dresses up in proper armour and knows how to fight with medieval weapons! He even lets us have a go!"

Mr Trevelyan saw the slightly worried look on Tia's face. "It's perfectly safe, Tia; don't worry. He'll just give you foam swords. You'll have to wait a few years before you can use the real thing!"

"It's still brilliant fun, though," Meghan clarified.

"But that's not what makes Mr Teague a brilliant teacher," Mrs Trevelyan cut in, eyeing Meghan and Mr Trevelyan with mock disapproval. "Your dad and I have known Mr Teague since we were all at university together. He's a very kind and caring man, and even back then it seemed as though he was made for teaching."

Images flashed through Tia's mind of Mr and Mrs Trevelyan when they were younger, meeting for the first time at university and getting to know each other. Many questions began to brew in her mind, but then she had questions brewing in her mind almost all the time, so it was a feeling she was very accustomed to. She decided to store them and many others away for another time, allowing the conversation to move on.

Tia struggled to fall asleep that evening. She was excited about her new school, but her excitement was always coated in a layer of anxiety. There was always a voice inside (somewhere around her stomach, as far as Tia could tell), warning her that the unknown was something to be feared.

Tonight, however, her mind was eager and her heart was happy, and the two joined forces to keep the fearful voice at bay, if not completely silent. Any further thoughts of her thirteen treasures and what her parents might be able to make of them were kept far from her mind.

At least for now.

Chapter Eleven

School

Tia would never have guessed Mr Teague was around the same age as her parents, but then she would have found it hard to guess his age at all. Tall and slim, he strode across the school lawn as if he still had plenty of youth left in him. But he also had the sort of big, bushy beard and grey-flecked hair that Tia would usually have associated with an older man.

He placed an arm on Meghan's shoulder. "Good morning, Meghan. It's good to see you again!" he said, embracing Mr and Mrs Trevelyan. "And this must be Tia." He squatted down so that his smiling eyes were level with hers, extending a similar welcome to her without presuming to invade her personal space. "I'm looking forward to all the adventures we're going to have this year," he said in a reassuring voice. Tia decided it was safe to return the smile.

Meghan quickly ran off with Bran, but Tia stuck close to Mr and Mrs Trevelyan, carefully surveying the scene. The school lawn was alive with cheerful chatter. Children and adults were busy catching up with friends after the long summer break, but a few other children had opted to stay close to their parents and just observe for the time being.

Tia caught sight of Pasco standing behind his frazzled mother, who was holding a crying twin in each arm while talking to a young woman with long blonde hair. Mrs Penrose had a slightly desperate look on her face and seemed to be trying to pass the wailing girls over to the blonde woman, who Tia assumed was their new teacher. Pasco glanced over in Tia's direction and smiled weakly. Tia smiled back and waved.

A bell rang from the top of the stone steps leading up to the school entrance at the side of the castle. Tia turned to see a mature but very fit-looking woman with short grey hair ringing the bell high in the air with one strong arm while holding a clipboard under the other.

Ms Morgan, she thought to herself.

"Good morning, wonderful people!" the woman bellowed joyfully at the crowds on the lawn, who had all ceased their conversations and turned their attention to her. The headteacher's eyes sparkled, and she grinned as if this gathering of children, parents and teachers was the most pleasing sight she had ever seen. Her voice matched her strong and energetic appearance.

"I hope you had a brilliant summer holiday and got plenty of rest because we have an exciting term ahead of us! Teachers, please gather your classes at the foot of the steps. Miss Williams will take the little ones straight over to the Longhouse on the other side of the lawn. If anyone is unsure which class they're in, please come to see me. Have a wonderful first day back, everybody!"

Ms Morgan had been walking down the steps as she spoke and had reached the grass by the time she finished speaking. She was instantly surrounded by children, some asking which teacher they were supposed to go to, but most simply recounting their summer adventures to her or asking about hers. She listened intently to each of them in turn, patiently resting a hand of acknowledgement on the shoulder of any children struggling not to interrupt the others with their own stories.

"Okay, Tia?" Mrs Trevelyan said, crouching down and taking Tia's hands in hers. "We'll both be here to meet you at the end of the day. You just take your time settling in. You're going to have a great time."

"Meghan's going to look out for you," Mr Trevelyan said, "but just tell her if she's crowding you at all."

They each gave her a kiss, which Tia was surprised not to find awkward at all, then she headed over to join the group that had assembled around Mr Teague. As she walked across the lawn, Pasco came alongside her.

"Are you nervous?" he asked.

"A little."

Tia's reply seemed to encourage him. "Me too," he sighed.

"Are your sisters okay?"

"I think they'll be all right. This is the first time they've been to school, plus we've only just moved here. I guess it's a lot of change all at once." Pasco's tone suggested that his sisters weren't the only ones struggling with the shift.

Once Mr Teague's class had gathered together, he announced that they weren't going inside straightaway but would play some games on the lawn instead. To begin with, they all sat on the grass in a circle and everyone took it in turns to say their name and how old they were. Twelve of them were already ten and had been in Mr Teague's class last year, while fourteen were the same age as Tia and Pasco, and were also new to the class. No one else had so recently moved to the village as Tia and Pasco, however, and they all seemed to know each other.

After this quick introduction they split into teams and played a game. Mr Teague called it Halo and said it was an ancient Celtic game that had been played all over Britain in pre-Roman times. It involved throwing a rubber ring over the end of a stick held by one member of each team at either end of the pitch. No one was allowed to move with the ring, so players had to pass it around to the rest of their team to get it closer to the stick without it getting intercepted by the other team. They were in three teams, and each team took it in turns to sit out for a game.

"The reason it was called Halo," Mr Teague explained to Tia and Pasco while their team was taking its turn to sit out, "is that a torc was originally thrown over a team member's head, like an angel's halo."

"What's a torc?" Tia asked. She wasn't entirely sure whether Mr Teague was being serious or not, but it was fun to play along.

"It's usually a ring made of gold, twisted like a thick, solid piece of rope in a circular shape that people would wear around their necks. You can imagine how dangerous throwing that at people's heads would be! Most games were played with iron torcs because iron was more readily available than gold, but it's also heavier and harder, so it would have made the game even more dangerous."

Tia laughed, but Pasco just looked at Mr Teague with a puzzled expression on his face. He clearly didn't know whether their teacher was being serious or not either, but it seemed more important to him to work out whether he was being told a historical fact or not.

It probably didn't help Pasco's enjoyment of the game that he was also pretty useless at it. Tia wasn't brilliant herself, but Meghan said afterwards that she had done really well for her first try, especially considering she was the shortest person in the class.

After several games of Halo the class headed inside to cool down. Tia had read a lot about castles, but this was the first time she had ever stepped inside such an old building.

On the other side of the huge doorway was a large room lined with benches and pegs, where all the children could hang up their bags and coats. Then they passed through a narrow passageway into the feasting hall, which was as bright as the passageway had been dark. Mid-morning light was streaming in through the huge windows that lined one wall, shining on three long wooden tables flanked by two long wooden benches apiece. The children took a seat at the nearest table and helped themselves to fruit juice from the metal jugs sitting on the tabletop.

Pasco, who seemed to have latched on to Tia as the only other newcomer, sat down to her right. She didn't mind, but he was even quieter than she was, and Tia didn't really want to have to make the effort in conversation all the time. They sat quietly and observed the others.

Tia looked up and down the table at her classmates. They all seemed to know each other well already and everyone was engaged in conversation. Meghan and Bran were standing at the end of the table having a heated discussion about an incident from the last game of Halo with two boys who were a head taller than Bran – even with the extra inches his curly hair gave him – and about twice as wide as Meghan.

"Rubbish!" Meghan exclaimed. "I caught it first and then you tried to yank it out of my hand! You're just a sore loser, Ivor Jones."

Ivor Jones growled at her and furrowed his large brow threateningly. His sidekick, who was possibly even a little taller and stouter, did the same in Bran's direction.

"Hello. Are you two new? I don't recognise you." A tall girl with short blonde hair and slightly sticky-out teeth sitting on the other side of Pasco had turned to talk to them. "Pasco and Tia, right? I'm Cerys."

"Hi. Yeah, we both just moved to Stormhaven." Tia thought Pasco wouldn't mind if she spoke for him as well. "Have you lived here long?"

"As long as I can remember," Cerys replied. "My mum and dad moved here soon after I was born. Mum writes books about British cultural identity in the Middle Ages and Dad runs the greengrocer's. What brought your families here?"

"My parents already lived here. I'm Meghan's sister."

The three of them turned to look at Meghan. She and Bran were now shoulder to shoulder with their arms folded, silently scowling at the two boys they had been arguing with.

"Oh, you're Meghan's new sister! And what do your parents do, Pasco?" Cerys asked.

"Mum's come here to be the school librarian."

"I expect we'll be seeing a lot of her, then. Mr Teague often gives us projects that involve quite a bit of research in the library. What about your dad?"

"He doesn't live with us any more." Pasco looked intently at the cup in his hands and Cerys shifted uncomfortably in her seat.

Tia had never thought about why Pasco's father wasn't with the rest of the family on either of the occasions she had seen them.

"Okay, everybody, let's head up to the classroom." Clearly sensing that Meghan and Bran's disagreement with the two large boys was approaching boiling point, Mr Teague had moved to stand between them before addressing the class.

Cerys seemed to appreciate the distraction and quickly hurried to the head of the crowd as the children moved towards the double doors at the other end of the hall.

Chapter Twelve

The Library

The classroom was at the top of a wide spiral staircase made of solid stone, and as Meghan had told Tia the day before, it was one of the castle's former bedchambers. Large pinboards on each of the walls displayed some of the previous year's work, and there was a well-stocked book corner complete with large beanbags. Several wooden tables and chairs of all different shapes and sizes were clustered around an enormous rug covered in a colourful spiral design that appeared large enough for all twenty-six of them to sit on together.

"Tia, Pasco, this is Aled." Mr Teague was walking over to them with a narrow-faced blond boy. "He's going to give you a quick tour of the school before lunch so you can get your bearings."

"I can take them, Mr Teague!" Meghan came rushing over excitedly.

"I expect Tia's had several tours around the sights of Stormhaven with you already this week, Meghan," Mr Teague said kindly, "and no doubt she'll have plenty more to look forward to. Why don't we let Aled show them around this time?"

Meghan looked disappointed but nodded, while Aled looked very pleased with himself for having been given such an important job. Tia gave Meghan a sympathetic smile as she and Pasco followed Aled out of the classroom.

The corridor outside led to two more large oak doors like the one guarding the entrance to their own classroom. All three were open, and the sound of children talking echoed off the stone walls and floor.

"These are the classrooms for the younger kids," Aled said in a slightly pompous voice, pointing to each of the doors in turn. "Earth class, Sea class and we're Sky class. And then the babies are out in the longhouse on the lawn."

They climbed a narrower spiral stone staircase up to another corridor containing more oak doors, though these were shut.

"This is the secondary school," Aled explained. "After Sky class with Mr Teague you move into Fire class for two years and you have Ms Morgan as your teacher. That's the class I'll be in next year." Aled's pointy chin seemed to stick out a little further and higher as he said this.

"You only have her as a teacher for some of the time, though. Because it's secondary school, you have a lot of new subjects with different teachers. Then after two years in Fire class you have a different teacher for every subject for the rest of your time at school."

They walked the length of the corridor and into an open circular room that Tia thought must be at the top of one of the towers. There were computers all along the outside wall, encircling two large cupboards standing back-to-back in the middle.

"This is the computer room."

Tia thought that much was obvious, but Aled was talking as though they were idiots and couldn't possibly know anything unless he told them.

"And through here is the library. The library's a labyrinth, and it takes up half the castle keep. We won't go round all of it, but let's go through here and down a couple of floors." Just before they walked the doorway, Aled spun around, looked intently at them, and added very seriously, "Stay close to me or you'll probably get lost."

Tia raised her eyebrows at Pasco once Aled had turned away, and Pasco suppressed a smirk. She wondered whether to tell their guide that Pasco was actually the librarian's son in the hope that it might take Aled down a peg or two, but she wasn't sure whether he would appreciate her drawing attention to him in such a way.

On the other side of the door was a dimly lit passageway. One side was lined with bookshelves, while old tapestries depicting battle scenes hung on the opposite wall. Tia glanced at the books, but the lettering was too faded to make out the titles in the murky light. At the end of the passageway they turned left into a similar corridor, only with old paintings along one wall rather than tapestries. Then they turned right, left and right again, down a narrow stone staircase and into another dark passage.

By this time, Tia was beginning to understand Aled's warning to stick close and Pasco was looking quite nervous. Then, all at once they turned another corner and found themselves on a balcony overlooking a sunlit hall, which was a mirror image of the feasting hall, with the same large windows. However, this vast room contained rows of bookshelves rather than tables and benches, and at the far end was a desk where a familiar figure sat.

"Hi, Mum!" Pasco's relief at emerging out of the library's tunnel-like corridors had made him a little light-headed, and he blushed following his impulsive shout. Tia smiled at him, but Aled frowned. He wore a puzzled expression as they descended a black spiral staircase to the floor of the great room.

"Hello, darling. How are you settling in?" Mrs Penrose got up from her desk and hurried over to meet them at the bottom of the staircase. She gave Pasco a big kiss on the cheek, which made him redden again.

"Yeah, fine," he said, looking anywhere but at Tia and rubbing his cheek as if worried his mother might have left an embarrassing mark. "We're just having a tour of the school."

"You didn't tell me you were the new librarian's son," said Aled, looking quite indignant that Pasco had withheld this information.

"Er, sorry," Pasco replied. He didn't really know how else to respond.

"How are *you* settling in, Mrs Penrose?" Tia asked.

"Okay, thank you, dear." She smiled kindly at Tia, as if she appreciated the concern. "I did get lost in the Middle Welsh literature section earlier, but I'm sure I'll be able to find my way around soon."

"We'd better get back over to the feasting hall for lunch," Aled said, somewhat sulkily.

Tia and Pasco said goodbye, then Aled marched them back to rejoin the rest of their class at one of the tables in the feasting hall.

The afternoon passed pleasantly. Mr Teague set them the task of writing about what they had done over the summer holidays, only they were to write accounts of two things that had really happened and a third that was fictitious.

"But try to make the false one as believable as possible," Mr Teague said, "and the true ones a bit far-fetched-sounding, so that someone reading them would have a hard time guessing which one isn't true."

Tia thought about recounting her escape from Mr Silverman the week before – that would certainly sound unbelievable, even though it was true – but decided against it. She also decided against describing the incident with the standing stone, as she fully expected Meghan to write about that. In the end she chose to recount some of her initial experiences of life at Stormhaven and the different places she had visited so far. She would think of a mundane place she hadn't visited as the fictitious account to fool her readers. Pasco, who was seated next to her at a table for four, was clearly having difficulty.

"I'm just not very good at writing fiction," he said. "It was easy to write the two true ones, but I'm not imaginative enough to just make stuff up."

Tia proposed that they each think of a third true thing that had happened to them over the summer and simply swap stories. This suggestion drew a huge sigh of relief from Pasco, and the pair set about finishing off the task.

"Tia," Pasco said quietly as the end of the day approached. "Do you think this is a proper school? I mean, it's a bit different from most schools, isn't it?"

Aled, who was sitting opposite them, looked

up. "Stormhaven Castle School of Exploration and Discovery is a *progressive* school," he said authoritatively. "That means it's *better* than most schools."

His tone was very pompous, but he blinked a little too much as he said this. Tia suspected he was trying to convince himself as much as them.

Tia didn't need much convincing, though. She looked around happily at her classmates, some of whom were sitting on beanbags, leaning against hardbacks in the book corner as they wrote their summer accounts. Others had clipboards and were sprawled out working on the rug, or sitting in the window seat chatting as they wrote. Rather than writing, Meghan seemed to be acting out the events of her summer holiday as she and Bran spoke excitedly to Mr Teague and to Ms Morgan, who had just popped in to see how everyone was doing.

"I love it," Tia said to Pasco.

"I like it too," he said, then leaned in closer for fear of being overheard again. "It's just that… do you think we're going to get a proper education? You know… to learn the things we need to pass exams and to know stuff for life in the real world."

Tia stared blankly at him for a few seconds, then smiled. Pasco was certainly a little odd, but she had made up her mind early on that they were going to be friends. Of all the many worries she had, this wasn't one of them. It was curious to meet such an anxious person, who was nervous about things Tia had hardly even considered.

"I think we're going to be okay, Pasco. Anyway, the real world can wait a while."

Chapter Thirteen

Exploration and Discovery

As the days passed, Tia became increasingly aware that she felt happy.

She hadn't exactly been *unhappy* before. Ms Davidson was kind, but she was so busy looking after all the girls in her care she had never really had time to give any of them more than basic care: healthy food, clean clothes, a roof over their heads and a positive outlook on life. As one of the quieter children, Tia had been left to cope with all the smaller things in life on her own, which meant they had often grown into larger things.

She had been accustomed to waking up in Ms

Davidson's house with a bubble of anxiety in her stomach as soon as she opened her eyes, which slowly grew throughout the day. She had always been worried about doing the wrong thing at school or getting on the wrong side of the older girls in the house, and she had constantly told herself to just keep her head down and get through the day.

It wasn't that she no longer felt the initial early morning anxiety; on the contrary, she did feel the familiar bubble. The difference now was that she had a greater bank of positive memories to call on to quell the churning in her stomach as each day passed. Memories of mealtime jokes with her father and sister; of afternoons reading on the sofa beside her mother; of evenings playing board games with her grandfather; of schooldays filled with exploration and discovery.

Before long, Tia was in complete agreement with Meghan's appraisal of Mr Teague as brilliant. Some days the class would drift into a seemingly empty classroom in the morning, only for Mr Teague to leap out of a cupboard dressed as a Victorian chimney sweep or the squire of a medieval knight. Then he would spend a couple of hours in character while the class asked him questions about the individual's life before writing up the interview.

One day he leapt out from behind a bookshelf dressed as a Viking raider, complete with an enormous double-headed axe, a blood-curdling battle cry and a fake plaited beard even wilder than his real beard, which reached down to his waist. The effect was so convincing that Rhea Bipul, the youngest in the class and barely taller than Tia, burst into tears. Mr Teague had to put away the axe, remove the fake beard and spend five minutes reassuring Rhea in his normal voice that he wouldn't scream again before he was able to continue with the lesson!

Sometimes they seemed to spend the entire day outside in the school grounds, measuring and mapping out the outbuildings as accurately as possible or cataloguing the various plant species. Twice they had taken out the foam swords and armour Meghan had told Tia about: once to re-enact the Battle of Hastings and once to illustrate medieval fighting techniques and emphasise the value of teamwork.

One Tuesday afternoon they had set off across the causeway, each with a large sketchbook under one arm, and entered a long workroom in the courtyard, where five or six objects that had been discovered in local archaeological digs had been spread out across the tables. The items included half a clay pot, a few metal farming tools and an ornamental brooch. The class had spent the afternoon trying to sketch them while Mr Teague and a couple of other archaeologists, including Mr Trevelyan, walked around talking to the children about how the objects had been used by their original owners.

Pasco's concerns about whether or not they were receiving a proper education gradually eased, but every so often he voiced a concern that Tia had never considered before and made her stop and think about how to reply sensitively without simply dismissing his fears.

"I mean, we haven't had a single maths or English lesson," he said after school one day at the end of September while they were sitting on the floor of her bedroom doing some homework, "or even numeracy or literacy. And we're a month into the term now! That can't be right, can it?"

"Think about what we've actually been doing, though," Tia said after a thoughtful pause. "I don't know about you, but I've definitely done more reading and writing than I did at my last school, and I think I've got better at it, too. And we've had to use maths a lot, like when we were making those graphs about how the population of Britain's changed in different areas over the centuries. Whenever we did maths at my old school we only ever seemed to do sums from a book. I never really thought it might actually be useful for something else."

"I guess so," admitted Pasco. "I'd still like to be told what I'm learning though; whether we're meant to be learning history or maths."

"You said you want to be prepared for life in the real world. Things aren't usually that clear cut in the real world, are they? Anyway, I like learning more than one thing at a time – it's way more fun. I never used to like doing stuff like reading through a bit of a story on a worksheet and circling the adjectives and adverbs in different colours. Who wants to just read part of a book? Either the bit they'd copied onto the worksheet was so dull I started thinking about something else, or it was so good I wanted to read the rest of the story."

"I was good at picking out adverbs."

Pasco sounded a little sulky, but Tia could tell he was thinking about what she'd said so she left it at that. She smiled to herself and went back to her colouring.

Mr Teague had asked them all to think of an important event in their lives and represent it in the style of the Bayeux Tapestry they had been learning about. They had started the exercise in class and were to complete it at home. Tia was putting the finishing touches to the second of three pictures showing her transition from Ms Davidson's house to Stormhaven. Pasco had also drawn two pictures. The first was of a family of five: Pasco, his little sisters and his mother and father. The second was almost identical, except that his father had disappeared and the remaining four looked considerably more sombre. Pasco was staring blankly at his pictures.

"Are you finished?" Tia asked.

"I know it's not very good. There isn't much going on, but I really don't know what else I could put in. Dad just left, and now there are only four of us."

This was the most Pasco had ever said about his parents' separation. Tia was interested to know more and felt it might be good for him to talk about it, but wasn't quite sure what to say.

"I think it looks great," Tia said encouragingly. "What are you going to do for the border?" Pasco shrugged and shook his head.

Mr Teague had explained that the border of the Bayeux Tapestry sometimes related symbolically to the action in the main section, but that most of the time it was either unconnected or the symbolism simply wasn't understood by anyone nowadays.

"Is there anything in particular you remember about your dad?" Tia asked. "Or about things you did together? Maybe you could draw some of the things that make you think of him."

Pasco looked at her thoughtfully for a few seconds, then nodded and picked up a pencil. After about twenty minutes they had both finished their drawings, so they showed each other what they had done. Pasco's border was a repeated pattern of a guitar, a book and an envelope.

"He was really musical," Pasco explained. "He sang these beautiful old songs in Cornish and Welsh. I couldn't understand a word of them, but he told me the stories behind them. He was really good at telling stories, too, so that's why I drew a book. Except he never read stories to me out of a book; he'd just retell them from memory. I drew a book because I didn't know how else to show it."

Tia didn't react, but she was quite surprised to hear this. She had expected Pasco's dad to be a librarian like his mother, or a scientist or something like that; certainly not a singer and storyteller. Pasco continued to stare at his picture. Tia remained very still, as if she were observing a timid creature that was carefully poking its nose out of its burrow and would be easily startled by any sudden movements.

"What about the envelope?" she said quietly.

"I get two letters from him a year: one at Christmas addressed to me and the girls – even though they hardly remember him now – and one for my birthday, which is just for me. That's it. He never gives his address and the postmark is never from the same town twice, so I have no way of contacting him. But he always seems to know what's going on in my life. Mum says Gran's in contact with him."

"What does he say in his letters?" Tia asked.

"Just a bit about what he's doing – mostly singing and playing in little pubs around the country, it seems – and he comments on whatever we've been up to. He always seems to end up telling a story about dragons or giants or knights on quests, though, and as I read it I can see him sitting on the edge of my bed telling it to me just like he used to." Pasco smiled to himself, then carefully tucked his drawing inside his bag. "What's yours about?"

Tia took that as a sign that he had said enough about his dad for now. She heard the front door open and shut again, which she assumed was Mr Trevelyan coming home from work. Meghan had gone to Bran's house for dinner, so it couldn't be her, and Mrs Trevelyan had walked home with them.

She looked down at her drawing and explained to Pasco how she had met her new parents and come to live in Stormhaven. After a slight pause for thought, Tia decided to tell him about the incident with Mr Silverman, and about the items she had been left with on Ms Davidson's doorstep, although she had not depicted these events in her life tapestry.

"Wow!" Pasco said. He had turned a little pale as Tia recounted her escape from Mr Silverman but was clearly fascinated by the mysterious items she had been left with as a baby. "So you have no idea what they mean?"

"No," she answered glumly. "Dad's seeing if he can find out anything about them. I'm pretty sure he and Mum have a theory, but I don't think they want to say anything until they know a bit more." Tia was just getting used to the idea of referring to the Trevelyans as Mum and Dad when talking to other people, though the words still felt a little strange to say and it still felt too awkward to use the names when speaking to them directly.

Mrs Trevelyan called Tia and Pasco downstairs for dinner. As they descended the stairs, the pair felt slightly more relaxed in each other's company than they had before, and Tia realised it was the first time she had spoken about her thirteen treasures to anyone other than her new parents.

As they walked past the living room door, Mr Trevelyan opened it. "Tia," he said softly, but with an undertone of urgency, "can I just have a quick word before dinner?"

Pasco suddenly seemed very self-conscious at the thought of having to make conversation with Mrs Trevelyan on his own, but Tia was anxious to hear what her father had to say. So, after giving Pasco a reassuring smile, she joined Mr Trevelyan in the front room.

"I got the final lab results today and wanted to let you know straightaway," he said quietly, "but I wasn't sure if you'd want me to talk about it in front of Pasco."

Mr Trevelyan motioned towards the coffee table, where the items Tia had given him to investigate a couple of weeks earlier were laid out; the very items she had just been talking about upstairs. It felt a little strange to see them again. It was like seeing one of the girls from Ms Davidson's home again; someone Tia had once been very close to but now seemed to belong to a different life.

Tia and her father sat down on the sofa.

"I'm sorry, Tia. I haven't been able to find out a great deal about them," he sighed, "but what I can tell you is that they're made of solid silver and I think they're about fifteen hundred years old. The twelve coins seem to be simply marked with crosses and circles, which no one I've spoken to can recall having seen before. We're not absolutely sure they're even coins. They might be some sort of token used for an unknown purpose." He paused and then picked up the pendant and chain in the same tender way that Mrs Trevelyan had handled them.

"The symbol on your pendant is called a Solomon's knot. It crops up in the artwork of various civilisations spanning from the Middle East to Ireland, as well as some ancient African cultures. It's been interpreted to mean a whole host of different things: eternity, love, wisdom and beauty, but always something very good."

He handed it back to Tia who, almost without thinking, fastened it around her neck again.

"The chain is only a few years old," he continued, "but the pendant is the same age as the coins. They're worth quite a lot, being solid silver and such old, mysterious objects. But I have no doubt that they're more valuable to you than any amount of money you could sell them for."

"So we don't really know anything more about why I was abandoned," Tia said in a hollow voice. It seemed silly now, but part of her had expected her father to crack some sort of code and to answer all of her questions, and she felt angry with herself for getting her hopes up.

"I'm sorry, Tia," Mr Trevelyan said, taking her

hand. "We're still trying to find out more about what Geoffrey Hemyke was working on when he died. We've made a lot of phone calls, but every time we track anyone down who might know a few details they seem quite fearful about telling us anything. Not only do people think he was murdered, but they also seem worried the culprits might come after them if they realised they knew something about it."

Tia picked up one of the coins lying on the table and turned it over in her hand. "When I first showed you these things it seemed as though you had an idea of what they might be about, but maybe you didn't want to tell me because you weren't sure." She looked up into her father's eyes and waited to see whether he would add anything.

"We really don't know anything for sure," he said cautiously, as if, even as he spoke, he was unsure whether or not to tell her, "but it did make your mum think of a particular legend Professor Hemyke may have been researching. Hemyke was an expert in the myths and legends of ancient Britain. Post-Roman Britain is your mum's field of expertise, so she knows a lot more about Hemyke than I do. We archaeologists tend to not be as knowledgeable about literature as historians."

He paused for a moment, then stood up to pace around the room a little before continuing. "She said the *number* of these objects brought to mind the legendary Thirteen Treasures of Britain. According to legend, it was a collection of different magical items Merlin had acquired from rulers and prominent people of the British kingdoms and hidden away. Each item is linked to a well-known king, lord or clergyman. The list includes a mixture of weapons, clothing and household items from the time, so nothing like your treasures. But the number of them and the fact this is something Hemyke would have worked on made your mother wonder whether he left these things as some sort of clue."

"She called these my 'thirteen treasures', but I don't understand what they have to do with me." Tia felt even more confused. It felt as if she had more questions than answers.

"I'm sorry, Tia," Mr Trevelyan said for the third time. "We really don't know either. That's why your mother didn't say anything. Until I can speak to someone who actually knows what Hemyke was working on, or we manage to get hold of his notes, I'm not sure we'll be able to work out exactly how you fit in.

"I'm going to a conference at the University of Wales in Aberystwyth in January. That's where Professor Hemyke worked, and it's also where the National Library of Wales is, so I think I may be able to find out more then. So far we've been able to identify the manuscripts he'd been researching at the library, and they were definitely the sort of documents you'd expect him to be looking at if he was working on something related to the legend of the Thirteen Treasures, but they could equally point to a whole host of other legends."

Mr Trevelyan put an arm around Tia and kissed her on the head. This took her by surprise, as did the fact that it made her feel a little better. Then she gathered up the coins and returned them to the little leather bag in her bedroom before joining everyone in the kitchen for dinner.

Pasco seemed relieved at her return.

"Okay, dear?" Mrs Trevelyan asked in a deliberate way, making it clear that she knew what Tia and her father had been talking about.

Tia just smiled and nodded in reply. She felt confused, but she could definitely say that she was okay. The effort her parents were making in trying to find explanations for her story meant more to her than any answers they might be able to come up with.

Chapter Fourteen

The Thirteen Treasures of Britain

Pasco and Tia went to the library after school the next day. They usually did this on days when Mrs Trevelyan wasn't working from home, as Tia preferred to read in the wonderful castle library than go home to an empty house.

After giving Mrs Penrose a brief report on how their day had been, they deposited their bags in the children's section, which consisted of several rows of low-level wooden bookcases painted all the colours of the rainbow and was situated along one side of the vast hall, beneath the great windows. A very dim grey light was filtering in through them that afternoon.

They had been set a project on games and recreation in the Middle Ages, which would take them up to the half-term break towards the end of October.

"I'm going to write something about board games, I think," said Pasco as he perused the titles on a bookcase decorated in red and green swirls. "I already know quite a bit about the history of chess, but I'd like to find out more about the games played in Europe before chess became really popular there. Are you okay, Tia?"

Pasco wasn't always the most observant of boys, but even he couldn't fail to notice that Tia's mind had been somewhere else all day. She was sitting on the floor, leaning against a radiator and staring intently at her outstretched feet.

"Tia?" Pasco waved a hand in front of her face, which finally got her attention. "What's up?"

Tia hadn't yet shared what Mr Trevelyan had told her the night before, but only because they hadn't had any time alone. She took the opportunity to bring him up to speed.

"The Thirteen Treasures of Britain," Pasco wondered aloud.

"Yeah," said Tia. "Have you heard of them?"

"No, but I bet there's a book in here that'll tell us a bit more about them."

Before long they had located a book called *The Encyclopaedia of British Myths and Legends.* Pasco searched the index for the relevant page.

"Here we are," he said. He began to read aloud from the book but soon stopped. "There are a lot of old Welsh names that I have no idea how to pronounce. Why don't we just read it to ourselves?" He turned the book so Tia could see it as well:

The Thirteen Treasures of Britain were a collection of items imbued with magical powers, which Merlin (Myrddin) acquired from prominent figures in Post-Roman Britain – mostly from what is now northern England but some from the South West and Wales – at the time of the Anglo-Saxon incursions into Celtic Britain. They included:

1) **The Sword of Rhydderch Hael.** If a worthy person drew it, it would burst into flames.
2) **The Hamper of Gwyddno Long-Shank.** Food for one man would be put inside it, but enough food for a hundred men would be found in it when reopened.
3) **The Drinking Horn of Bran the Stingy.** Whatever drink might be wished for would be found inside it.
4) **The Chariot of Morgan the Wealthy.** If a man rode in it, he would quickly find himself wherever he wished to be.
5) **The Halter or Bridle of Clydno Eiddyn.** He would find whichever horse he might wish for in the halter.

6) **The Knife of Llawfrodedd the Horseman.** This would serve enough meat for twenty-four men to eat at the table, multiplying the food as it was cut.

7) **The Cauldron of Dyrnwch the Giant.** If meat for a coward were put inside it to boil, it would never boil. But if meat for a brave man were put inside, it would boil quickly, thus distinguishing the brave from the cowardly.

8) **The Whetstone of Tudwal Tudglyd.** If a brave man sharpened his sword against it, it would defeat anyone he fought. If a cowardly man sharpened his sword against it, his sword would be rendered useless.

9) **The Coat of Padarn Red-Coat.** If a noble man put it on, it would be the right size for him; if the man were dishonourable, it would not fit.

10) and 11) **The Pot and the Dish of Rhygenydd the Cleric.** Whatever food might be wished for would be found in them.

12) **The Chessboard of Gwenddolau.** If the pieces were set in their starting places, they would play by themselves. The board was made of gold, the men of silver.

13) **The Mantle of Arthur in Cornwall.** Whoever was covered by the hooded cloak could not be seen, though he could see everyone.

"That's a pretty weird list of things," said Tia. "Is there anything else?"

"Yeah. It says that when Merlin first asked the various owners for these treasures they said they would only give them to him if he could first obtain the Drinking Horn of Bran the Stingy. They thought this would be impossible, but he did manage to get the horn – which was supposedly removed from the head of a centaur Hercules defeated – and so he received them all."

Tia sighed. "I still don't understand how any of this has anything to do with me. None of this stuff is even real, is it? I mean, King Arthur and Merlin weren't real people, were they?"

"Loads of these old stories sound like that," Pasco said thoughtfully. "I remember one time my dad had just told me an incredible story about King Arthur and his knights battling an army of men who had the heads of dogs, and I was saying how crazy and made up that was. He said: 'Legends may be born from half-forgotten memory or half-understood experience, but they're never made up out of thin air, and sometimes there's more truth in legend than in fact.' "

Pasco frowned hard at nothing in particular as he spoke, as if it felt uncomfortable for him to recall his father so vividly.

"He meant that even the weirdest legends are based on something that really happened, and he told me how some warriors believed they could call on the spirits of animals like wolves to make them look fiercer. They would wear wolfskins with the wolf's head as a hood." He shut the book and smiled at Tia. "If the legend has something to do with your past, I think we should find out as much as we can, even if we don't find the answers we want, and even if it turns out to have nothing at all to do with you. It's worth a try."

Perhaps it was the way he had said 'we', but something made Tia throw her arms around Pasco's neck.

"Thank you!" she said tearfully.

"Er, you're welcome," he said stiffly, nervously checking that no one, and especially not his mother, could see them.

Chapter Fifteen

The Intruder

A fine drizzle had already begun to fall, and the loitering dark clouds promised heavier rain to come as Tia made her way home with her mother through a chilling wind blowing in from the sea. Mrs Trevelyan had come to the library having finished whatever work it was she had been doing in the courtyard, and she now held the large umbrella over the two of them as they hurried through the narrow streets of the village. It looked as though this would be the night that autumn arrived in force.

Tia had borrowed *The Encyclopaedia of British Myths and Legends* from the library. Even without the weight of the book in her backpack reminding her, she would have found it hard to think of anything other than the things she had begun to discover about the legend of the Thirteen Treasures of Britain in the last twenty-four hours.

"Do you think King Arthur was a real person?" she asked her mother abruptly as they turned down a street with a row of terraced houses on each side, which gave them slight shelter from the gusty wind.

"Why do you ask that?" Mrs Trevelyan said, looking at Tia with an expression of mild surprise on her face.

It might have been a bit of a strange question for her to come out with at that moment, but it felt like a natural link in the chain of thoughts that had been forming in Tia's head.

"Dad said most of the Thirteen Treasures of Britain were supposed to belong to real and important people," Tia said, trying to explain her thought process and only stumbling a little over her utterance of the word 'dad' this time. "But one of them is thought to be a cloak that belonged to King Arthur and I didn't think he was a real person. Dad also said you knew lots about the history of Britain."

"Did he?" she said, grinning. "Well, personally I think there must have been an Arthur-like person around AD 500 who united lots of the tiny Celtic kingdoms. He was probably a great warrior who led an army of horse-mounted soldiers in battles across a large area when the Saxons were moving westward into Celtic lands. That's probably where the legends about

Arthur's knights come from. But I think it's unlikely he was ever king of all Britain in the way the later legends suggest. The best-known legends were written several hundred years after the time an Arthur figure would have lived, and the writers placed the events within their own cultural context, which was very different from the world of AD 500."

Tia just about understood this explanation, but was beginning to realise how little she really knew about so many things.

"When we get in, I'll dig out a map and try to explain it a bit better," her mother said reassuringly.

They turned a corner into their street and could see Meghan ahead of them, crouching down on the doorstep to peer through the letterbox.

"Oh, there you are," she said as they approached. "I thought I could hear you inside already, but the door was locked."

"You look absolutely soaked through, and your jeans are filthy," said Mrs Trevelyan as she rummaged through her bag in search of the key.

"I've been playing *gameball* with Bran," Meghan said excitedly.

Tia could have sworn Meghan had picked out a red headscarf with white spots to hold her hair back that morning, but the one she was now wearing appeared to be brown with greyish spots.

"Mr Teague has set us a project to research a

medieval game," continued Meghan, "and we're going to do gameball, which is like an ancient version of football but a bit like rugby, too. No one really knows what the rules were – or even if there were any rules – so we're going to do some experiments and come up with our own."

"Well, maybe you could change into some shorts for your next experiment," Mrs Trevelyan said as she turned the key in the door.

As the front door swung open, a dark shape flashed before them and dashed down the hallway into the kitchen.

"Hey!" yelled Meghan. "Stop!" She dropped her schoolbag and sprinted into the house.

"Meghan, no!" Mrs Trevelyan screamed, immediately running after her.

Tia instinctively followed them.

It was clear now that the dark shape was a slight and very agile person dressed in dark clothes, including a black balaclava, and clutching a small black bag in one hand. The figure was running noiselessly through the kitchen towards the back door, which stood wide open.

Meghan wasn't far behind the shadowy figure and Mrs Trevelyan followed closely after her, each yelling at the person ahead of them to stop.

One after another they burst out into the drizzly evening air. Tia saw the dark figure leap onto the stile over the hedge at the top of the garden, pause to get its balance and then jump down on the other side while her sister and mother ran up the steps that ascended the terraced rear garden in hot pursuit.

"Stop!" Meghan yelled again.

To Tia's surprise, the masked figure stopped dead this time, just the other side of the stile. And then she saw why. Grandpa Locryn stood blocking the path that ran up towards the chapel, a thunderously threatening look on his face.

The intruder glanced at Meghan, then briefly back at Grandpa Locryn before hurling the bag at Grandpa Locryn's face and sprinting past as his arms shot up to catch it. Realising what was happening just a little too late, Grandpa Locryn turned sharply to pursue the swiftly disappearing figure, but he slipped on the wet ground and his chance was lost.

"Meghan, stop!" Mrs Trevelyan grabbed hold of Meghan's waistband as the impetuous girl tried to clamber over the stile, and the two of them fell backwards in a heap.

"But Mum, he's getting away!"

"You mean *she's* getting away," said Grandpa Locryn as he climbed over the stile and helped them to their feet. "I may not be able to describe her any more than to say that she was five foot six with dark eyes, but that was definitely a woman." He handed the black cloth bag the intruder had thrown at him to Tia while he rummaged in his pocket for his phone. "Can you hang on to that while I call Constable Pengully? Let's get in out of this rain." He scrolled through the contacts on his mobile as they headed into the kitchen.

"Why didn't you let me catch her?" Meghan asked her mother disappointedly as she sunk into a kitchen chair sulkily.

"She might have been dangerous," Mrs Trevelyan replied as she filled up the kettle from the kitchen tap with trembling hands. Meghan made a grumpy noise but made no attempt to argue.

"Come on, Tia, let's go round the house and see if anything's been stolen."

Meghan clearly needed to do something constructive, so Tia followed her out of the kitchen, still unconsciously clutching the burglar's bag that everyone seemed to have forgotten in the excitement.

"Try not to move anything," Grandpa Locryn called down the hallway after them. "The police will want to search for clues."

The girls passed the open door to the living room, which looked untouched, then climbed the stairs and peered inside their parents' bedroom. This room appeared to have been searched. The wardrobe doors were wide open and several drawers had been pulled out of their mother's dressing table, the contents of which had been emptied onto the bed.

The girls turned and ventured into their own bedroom at the front of the house. The room – especially Meghan's half – had been a little untidy when they left for school that morning, but it now looked like a bombsite. Every drawer had been pulled out and their clothes were strewn across the floor, muddled with every book that had previously occupied the bookshelves. Even their mattresses had been tipped up. The intruder had clearly wanted to discover every potential hiding place in the room. The girls stared about them, rooted to the spot for a few seconds.

"We didn't leave the room looking *this* bad, did we?" Meghan asked after a while.

"No," Tia confirmed.

"Mum!" called Meghan as she turned and ran back downstairs.

Staring at her upturned mattress, and thinking of what she kept hidden under there, Tia's hand instinctively moved towards the pendant around her neck. Then she reached into the bag she had forgotten she was holding. Searching inside, her fingers closed around the only item it contained and pulled it out.

It was the small, familiar leather pouch containing her twelve silver coins.

"Tia," called Grandpa Locryn. "The constable's asking if the burglar managed to pop anything inside the bag before you disturbed her. Is there anything in it?"

Tia froze, and a basic, fear-driven instinct to hide took over. "No," she called back. "It's empty."

Chapter Sixteen

The Leader of Battles

For some reason she couldn't quite explain, Tia didn't tell anyone what the burglar had attempted to steal from the house. She simply slipped the leather bag into her pocket and the police took away the empty black cloth bag as evidence, supposing the intruder had been disturbed before she had been able to steal anything.

"It's a bit strange she went through the kids' room so thoroughly, though," Constable Pengully had said, scratching his flabby chin absentmindedly. "That was probably the least likely room to contain anything of value, like money or jewellery."

"She might've been after small electrical items," suggested Constable Rowe, the younger and far scrawnier of the two policemen tasked with the usually straightforward task of keeping the peace in Stormhaven.

The bag was the only clue they had been able to find, and no one had been seen crossing the causeway, which meant the mysterious intruder was either hiding out on the island or was a resident. Both possibilities were unsettling.

Once the police had finished at the house, Grandpa Locryn had taken the girls to the Green Man's Bear, one of the three village pubs, where he had a skittles match lined up. He had been coming to the house to ask if they wanted to cheer him on, and suggested taking Meghan and Tia there for dinner to give their parents time to process what had happened.

Tia sat quietly, picking at her food with one hand as she watched the skittles game, her other hand alternately checking that her treasures were still in her pocket and her pendant was still around her neck. Her eyes darted towards the door every time someone came in.

Meghan didn't appear to be remotely traumatised by the break-in. In fact, she seemed delighted to have a new story to dramatically recount to anyone who wasn't able to walk away quickly enough.

On the Sunday afternoon a couple of days later, Tia had just about worked up the courage to tell her parents what she had hidden from the police on the evening of the break-in. She checked that the bag and its coins were in her pocket – despite the fact they hadn't been out of her pocket since the incident – and went downstairs to talk to her parents while Meghan was out conducting more gameball experiments with Bran.

She found them in the kitchen with a large map of Britain spread out on the table.

"Ah, Tia," Mrs Trevelyan said, seeing her enter the room. "I just remembered I was going to tell you a bit more about the historical 'King' Arthur the other night before all that nasty business. Come and have a look at this map."

Tia decided her confession could wait, and went to stand between her parents so she had a good view.

"You know the Romans occupied Britain for a few hundred years, don't you?" her mother began.

Tia nodded.

"Well, by the fifth century the Roman Empire was crumbling, and eventually all their troops were withdrawn to defend Rome against invaders, leaving Britain to the Celtic British tribes."

"The culture would still have had a definite Roman influence," Mr Trevelyan said, "but it was also very Celtic. Christianity would have been the major religion, but it was probably practised in a uniquely Celtic way by most people, such that many Christian Romans from the continent would have considered the British people to be pagans and barbarians."

Mrs Trevelyan noticed the strained look on Tia's face as she tried to keep up and directed her attention back to the map. "Soon after the Romans left, the Saxons and other people from Northern Europe started coming across and landing in the east of what is now England." She ran a finger down and around the coast from Yorkshire to the Isle of Wight.

"People used to think this was an aggressive invasion right from the start," Mr Trevelyan said, "but there isn't really any archaeological evidence to support this."

"You mean the Celtic people just let them move in?" Tia asked.

"Kind of," he said. "Britain was like a new world of opportunity for the Saxons; not too hot or cold, and with lots of space. And we're talking about a very gradual process over many years. In time they intermarried with the local Celtic Brits as well as other immigrant people groups, such as the Angles and Jutes. But this is all happening almost exclusively in the east of the island." Mr Trevelyan made a chopping motion with his hand more or less down the middle of England and swept it away to his right to indicate where this Anglo-Saxon part of the country lay. "Britain was still very much a Celtic land in the west and in Scotland."

"Then in around AD 500 we start to see a lot of

records of battles as the Anglo-Saxons move westwards," Mrs Trevelyan said. "Unlike their initial landings, it seems this was very much an aggressive invasion, which the Celtic people ferociously fought against. There seems to have been a definite divide between the Celts in the west and the Anglo-Saxons (who also still had a lot of Celtic blood) in the east, but we don't really know how united each of these groups was. It's unlikely that this was simply a war between two large, organised nations. And it's from within this context that we see a historical Arthur figure emerging."

"But he wasn't a king, was he?" Tia asked, remembering her initial conversation with her mother.

"Not exactly," her mother continued. "The whole country was made up of tiny kingdoms and tribal territories, which had a long history of fighting among themselves. Arthur may well have been lord of one of the Celtic territories, but the earliest references call him a 'leader of battles'. Arthur was, first and foremost, a great warrior who united the feuding Celtic British people against a common enemy."

"And he won?" Tia asked.

"It seems that way," Mrs Trevelyan said, "though it was a temporary victory. Arthur is recorded as having enjoyed twelve great victories against the Saxons, and it sounds as though there was peace for about fifty years after the twelfth. Following that, the Saxons eventually pushed the frontier further back so that Scotland, Wales and Cornwall were the only regions in Britain that were inhabited solely by Celtic Britons, but this Anglo-Saxon advance took centuries, and the Celtic peoples would largely have been absorbed into a new 'English' people group, which was Angle, Saxon, Jute and Celtic all woven together, rather than completely eradicated. A bloody Saxon conquest of the Celtic tribes was avoided, thanks to Arthur's victories."

Tia's head was bulging with all this information. She just about understood what had been said, but there wasn't room for any more information for the time being. She sighed and sat down in a chair, staring at the map and visualising the movements of Celtic and Anglo-Saxon armies across the country. The important thing was that Arthur, and therefore his cloak, could well be historical fact after all, which meant there might still be some truth behind the legend of the Thirteen Treasures of Britain, which her own treasures seemed to point towards.

"Who'd like a hot chocolate?" Mr Trevelyan asked brightly.

Tia's parents sensed that she couldn't take in any more history that night.

Before long, they were each seated at the kitchen table with a mug of steaming hot chocolate complete with melting marshmallows. It was raining heavily outside, and cradling something so warm and sweet-smelling felt very satisfying.

"I hope Meghan and Bran have gone inside," Mrs Trevelyan sighed, gazing out of the window.

I'll tell them about the burglar stealing my coins another day, Tia thought as she slurped contentedly from her mug.

Chapter Seventeen

Where Real Truth Lies

Over the next two weeks, everyone in Sky class became increasingly engrossed in their medieval pastimes projects. Aled and another older boy called Dafydd were researching archery, trying to make the rest of the class understand that this had been by far the most important pastime for people living in the Middle Ages. When two younger boys told them they had chosen bowls as their game, Aled and Dafydd were quick to tell them it had at one time been outlawed so the peasants could spend more time practising their archery. Mr Teague had to swoop in and reassure the younger boys that bowls was still a perfectly good choice of topic.

Nessa and Tamsyn, two girls of Tia's age who considered themselves to be fairy-tale princesses, had chosen to look at medieval embroidery, as needlework had been a major pastime for noble ladies. Ivor Jones and his equally thuggish friend 'Gareth the Butcher', who happened to be the son of the village butcher, wanted to bring in dead animals for their presentation on medieval hunting, but Mr Teague suggested that might not be appropriate.

He also intervened to prevent Meghan and Bran going outside on their own during schooltime to conduct gameball experiments. They had to save those for the weekend and work on writing up their presentation instead. Everyone was to make a short presentation to the rest of the class on the last Friday before half-term. The prospect had sucked a lot of the enjoyment out of the project for Pasco until Tia asked if she could partner with him on his medieval board game project as she hadn't found anything particularly enticing to explore.

Tia was finding it hard to think about anything aside from the Thirteen Treasures legend. At first she had wanted to focus on horse riding, as a couple of the treasures in the legend – the bridle and the chariot – related to horses, but Talwyn Cornish had chosen horse riding. Talwyn knew much more than Tia about horses, seeing as her father ran the pony-trekking stable in Appleketh, the tiny hamlet just beyond the castle on the mainland.

Board games seemed like the next best choice, given that one of the Thirteen Treasures was a chessboard. Chess didn't have quite the same appeal as horses, but at least she would be working with Pasco.

One windy afternoon in mid-October while they were sheltering in the library after school, he said: "I've been thinking about something, Tia. I don't see how a chessboard could be one of the Thirteen Treasures of Britain."

Tia looked up from *The Encyclopaedia of British Myths and Legends* she had been flicking through with a slightly startled expression on her face. "What do you mean?" she asked.

Tia had invested a great deal of thought and emotion in this mysterious tale. She needed to believe there was some truth or meaning to it because, in her mind, it seemed so entwined with her own thirteen treasures.

Pasco knew how important it was to her and had clearly been working up the courage to voice this thought. "I'm not saying the whole legend is rubbish," he clarified hastily. "It's just that chess didn't reach Britain until hundreds of years after the time Merlin would have gathered the treasures together."

Tia could think of no explanation for this and felt a hollow sensation beginning to grow in her stomach. It was all just made up… of course it was! How could she have been so stupid? It had sounded ridiculous right from the start. Geoffrey Hemyke was clearly just a crazy old man, and she was better off not knowing what her connection to him might be. Was there any link at all anyway? She figured that just because there were thirteen of them didn't necessarily mean someone was leaving a clue to the ancient legend.

She closed *The Encyclopaedia of British Myths and Legends* and tossed it to one side, feeling as though she was throwing away a mooring line and letting herself drift into uncertainty once more.

"I'm sure it's just that the book simplified the legend a bit," Pasco said, looking increasingly uncomfortable. "I'll go and see if my mum knows about any other books that mention the Thirteen Treasures." He picked up the discarded encyclopaedia and hurried off to find Mrs Penrose.

Tia sat on her own, staring into space. Tears began to well in her eyes, and she felt angry with herself for getting all emotional about something so silly. But getting frustrated just made her tears fall all the faster.

"Ah, there you are, Tia." Mrs Trevelyan's voice sounded as though it was coming from a long way away. "Are you ready to –"

The sight of her daughter crying silently in the corner stopped Mrs Trevelyan in her tracks. She put her bag down on the floor, sat down next to her daughter and wrapped the small girl up in her arms. Tia buried her face into her mother's neck and cried for a few minutes before trying to explain, between continued sobs, why she was upset.

"I know it's stupid to get upset about it, but –"

"It's not at all stupid," Mrs Trevelyan interrupted. "You have a gap in your history that you want to understand. Anyone would! Our understanding of who we are depends on our understanding of where we've come from. Finding out about this legend has helped you begin to accept who you are, even if it hasn't given you factual answers, like where you were born or who your birth parents were."

"But it was silly to think the legend would be so important to understanding who I am," Tia protested. "We don't have a clue how it's connected to me!"

"We have plenty of *clues*, Tia," her mother said gently. "What we don't have is an explanation of all the clues. But even without a nice simple explanation, and even with all the knowledge gaps we've still got, you've started to find meaning in your story that you didn't have before. So of course it's upsetting to feel as though that meaning's being challenged."

Tia dried her eyes on her sleeve. There was still a hollowness inside her, but she was no longer angry with herself for feeling that way.

"I've got it, Tia! Oh, hi there, Mrs Trevelyan." Pasco had returned holding an impressive-looking old book, but he stopped short at the sight of Mrs Trevelyan consoling a crying Tia. He shifted uncomfortably. "I think I upset Tia," he said quietly, then turned to face Tia. "I'm sorry."

Tia smiled at him through slightly puffy eyes. "You don't need to apologise, Pasco. What is it you've found?"

Pasco breathed a sigh of relief. "This," he said holding up the large book.

The main title seemed to be written in a foreign language, but below it, in slightly faded lettering, Tia could make out the words *The Triads of Britain*. He knelt down on the floor in front of them and opened the book. Each page seemed to be split in two down the middle, with one side written in the same strange language as the title and the other in English.

"The earliest records of the Thirteen Treasures are written in Welsh, and in Welsh the chessboard treasure is called a gwid-bill or something like that." Pasco said this last word very slowly, reading it from the page and frowning as he did so.

"Can I see?" Mrs Trevelyan pulled the book towards her, keeping one arm around her daughter's shoulders. "*Gwyddbwyll*. I think it's pronounced more like g'with-b'wihl."

Tia and Pasco tried, but they couldn't work out how to make the sound of the double 'L' at the end of the word.

"Never mind," Mrs Trevelyan said, pushing the book back towards Pasco. "Carry on with what you were saying, Pasco."

"Okay. Gwid-bill *is* the Welsh word used for modern chess, but it was also the name of an ancient Celtic board game. By the time chess made it to Wales, the rules of the ancient game had been forgotten by most people, so they just used the same Welsh word as the name for chess. No one knows how the original was played nowadays, but there was definitely a board game – probably very different from chess – called gwid-bill around in the sixth century, and I think that's what this chessboard treasure actually was."

"So the Thirteen Treasures might have been real?" Tia said cautiously.

"Well, I'm not sure about all the magical properties they were supposed to have, but remember what my dad told me about there sometimes being more truth in legend than in history."

"I might use that line in my next paper, Pasco!" Mrs Trevelyan said, looking very impressed. "And that's some excellent research you've just done there."

Pasco turned pink.

Perhaps it was just to spare Pasco's blushes, but Mrs Trevelyan shifted her attention to her daughter. She spoke gently but seriously: "Tia, every philosophical, scientific or historical theory ever thought up is basically just someone's best explanation of the clues they see before them. Don't ever be afraid to put your faith in something that gives meaning to your experience and feelings. But stay open-minded and always be prepared to let your beliefs be challenged. That's where real truth lies."

Tia buried her face in her mother's neck once again, but this time without any tears.

Feeling as though he was intruding a little, Pasco went off to return *The Triads of Britain* to his mother.

Just as she had when she ran straight from Mr Silverman's clutches into her mother's arms, Tia felt safer than she ever had before.

Chapter Eighteen

Black Ravens

As Tia reflected back on that windy afternoon in the library over the next day or two, a couple of odd things struck her that she hadn't thought of at the time.

"Can you speak Welsh?" she enquired of her mother the following day as they washed up the breakfast bowls.

"I can't speak it very well," Mrs Trevelyan replied with a laugh, "but you can't be a historian of Sub-Roman Britain without being able to read a bit of ancient Welsh. Sub-Roman Britain is what we call the period immediately after the Romans left," she said in response to Tia's confused expression. "Most of the earliest British literature was in Welsh. A few histories and things may have been written in Latin, but all the poetry and stories, which I find much more informative, are in Welsh."

The other odd thing that struck her was how knowledgeable Pasco seemed to have been about the game of gwyddbwyll.

"It's what we're doing our project on, isn't it? Medieval board games." Pasco seemed a little embarrassed when she raised the subject one Saturday afternoon and avoided making eye contact.

"It is," said Tia, "but I'm doing the project with you, and I don't remember coming across any ancient Celtic board games." She had gone over to Pasco's house to work on it, as there was less than a week to go before the class presentations.

"I guess it is a bit obscure," said Pasco, pretending to look for a very particular pencil in his pencil case. "It's interesting, though, because nobody really has any idea how it was played. A lot of people think it was related to tafl games, but nobody really knows."

"What's tafl?"

It was becoming apparent that Pasco had done a lot more research into this board games project than he was letting on.

"Tafl's the name given to a whole bunch of games played in Scandinavia and the British Isles," he said. "There are a few different stories that explain the set-up behind all these games – like a king trying to escape from a burning castle under siege, surrounded by the enemy or a nobleman and his squires cornered in the forest by bandits – but the basic idea is that you have a king and his defenders in the middle of the board, trying to win by escaping to the edge or the corners, and the attackers around the outside of the board trying to win by capturing the king."

"Why aren't we mentioning this in our presentation?" Tia asked.

"I thought it might be too much to talk about with all the other games we're covering," Pasco said in a small voice.

"Then let's cut something else out," said Tia, becoming slightly exasperated. "This sounds more interesting than chess – everybody's heard of that. Come on," she said encouragingly, "tell me more about this game. Could we give a demonstration, or does it take too long to play?"

"Well, there are quite a few different versions of it. There's Hneftafl –"

"Bless you!" said Tia with a laugh.

"Very funny," said Pasco. "That would probably take a long time to play, though, and Tablut wouldn't be much better. Ard Ri might be good – that version was played in Scotland and used a smaller board with fewer pieces – but the Irish version Brandubh would probably be the best to use for a quick demonstration. The name means 'black raven' in Irish."

"Great," said Tia, trying not to look too taken aback

at the amount of information Pasco was able to store in his head. "How do you play it?"

Pasco hesitated for a moment. "It's such an ancient game that nobody really knows for sure. There are hardly any records that describe the full rules of most tafl games. Brandubh was played on a seven-by-seven square board, and they're pretty sure about the number of pieces on each side, but after that it's guesswork, really."

"That's okay," said Tia encouragingly. "We can try out a few rules and decide what works best. We can make notes and tell everyone how the different rules worked out. That's basically what Meghan and Bran have done for their whole project."

Pasco liked the sound of this. He rummaged around in a cupboard for his chess set. Once he had found it he picked out the white king, four white pawns and all of the eight black pawns. Then he blocked off one row and one column of the board to make a seven-by-seven grid by laying down two pieces of paper. Once this was done, the two friends set about experimenting with different rules.

By the time Mrs Penrose called upstairs to say dinner was ready, they had decided to ditch most of the presentation material written up so far so they could introduce the various types of tafl game and present the results of their Black Raven experiments.

The medieval pastimes presentations took place in the afternoon on the last Friday before half-term. Tia and Pasco were up second, which Tia was glad about because Pasco looked so nervous she thought he might throw up. Their demonstration of Brandubh went down very well. They had decided to do it using members of the class as the pieces, marking out the board on the classroom floor with lengths of rope.

When it was over, Pasco collapsed into a chair beside the window with a huge sigh of relief. Tia could also feel herself relaxing too, and she almost fell asleep during Nessa and Tamsyn's embroidery presentation.

Several people *did* fall asleep when Aled and Dafydd droned on about archery for nearly half an hour. On reflection, Tia thought it was something of an achievement the way they managed to suck every last drop of excitement out of what should have been quite an interesting topic, rendering it more mundane than a needlework explanation. Meghan and Bran were up last, and, as their presentation required them all to be outside, Mr Teague asked everyone to gather up their things ready to go straight home once the gameball presentation was over.

Tia was a little surprised to discover how hard Meghan and Bran had worked. She knew they had spent a lot of time 'experimenting' with rule variations, but she had imagined them just kicking a ball to each other and arguing. Once the class was gathered outside in the mercifully mild October afternoon air, Meghan and Bran gave a brief introduction to describe how they had developed the rules for the game. Although they weren't working from a script and ended up interrupting each other several times, it was clear that they had done a great deal of research.

The class spent the last half-hour before the week-long school holiday laughing and running around together as they played a spot of gameball for themselves. The game was basically football with a couple of variations that made for a very different game. Players were allowed to use their hands to catch the ball but weren't allowed to throw the ball or run with it. There were no goalkeepers, but there was an area around each goal that no one was allowed to enter, so players had to shoot from a distance. Tackling seemed to be the main area where the rules needed to be clarified a little further.

"Ivor Jones, you can't tackle someone like that!" Meghan yelled after the boy in question had charged headlong into Bran, sending him flying through the air.

Bran sat up with a grimace before trying to assume a casual, indifferent expression, as if he had intended to sail through the air with his limbs flailing before landing in a heap. His mouth seemed to form around the words "I'm fine", but the only sound that came out was a squeaky wheeze.

Meghan grabbed one of Bran's hands and hauled him to his feet, still scowling at Ivor.

"Sorry," Ivor said, grinning unashamedly at his sidekick, Gareth the Butcher.

Meghan stomped off towards the two large, square boys, her face turning a deeper and more furious shade of red with every step. Unfortunately for Bran, he had been leaning on Meghan for support while clutching his stomach and gasping for breath. As she stormed off, he promptly toppled over and thudded back down to the ground.

"All right, everybody," said Mr Teague, quickly forming a physical barrier between Meghan and Ivor once again. "I think we'll stop there. You're just winded, Bran. It'll wear off soon. Have a wonderful week off, everyone!"

Chapter Nineteen

The Goat-fish

The first few days of Tia's half-term break were wonderful indeed. After a relaxing weekend at home, Mrs Trevelyan had the Monday off work and took her and Meghan to see the smugglers' hoard they had discovered at the Jamaica Inn Smugglers Museum on Bodmin Moor. Mr Trevelyan had Tuesday off and took them to the Museum of Somerset, where the Roman figurine they had found was on show.

It was a little surreal to think they had discovered this weird and wonderful object that the best historians and archaeologists at Stormhaven were struggling to explain. Tia remembered what her mother had said about theories being people's best guesses based on the clues they had before them, and her imagination quickly began to conjure up explanations of its own.

Perhaps the Roman general who had led the conquest of Britain was presented with the figurine by Caesar, brought it back to Britain and kept it on his desk as a paperweight. Then it was stolen by British rebels, who kept it as a trophy to show that it was possible to stand up to the might of Rome. Then it was lost for centuries until a farm boy dug it up while he was ploughing a field. He joined a pirate crew, which terrorised trade ships along the Cornish coast and hid it with his plunder in the labyrinthine tunnels of Stormhaven.

"This is so cool!" Meghan said in an awed voice as she gawped at the figurine in the display case.

She had told the man at the reception desk that they had come to see a treasure they had discovered. Tia had been glad there was no one else in the room at that moment or Meghan would no doubt have re-enacted the whole story for them.

Their parents had to work for the rest of the week, although Mrs Trevelyan was able to work from home quite a bit and Grandpa Locryn came over every day.

"I bumped into Dougal Dinsmore this morning," their grandfather told them over lunch on the Friday. "He said he'd like the two of you to pop over and see him this afternoon if you can."

"Professor Dinsmore?" Meghan said, looking confused. "Why does he want to talk to us?"

"Said he had something to show you."

Dougal Dinsmore's office was in one of the whitewashed buildings that populated the castle courtyard. In the middle of his wooden door was a small rectangular patch of slightly darker wood, indicating there had once been a small plaque screwed to it. In its absence, someone had simply written the words 'Dougal Dinsmore: Project Leader' in black marker pen.

Meghan lifted her hand to knock but stopped when she heard raised voices coming from within.

"It's out of the question, Llacheu! It would be a dagger in the heart of this community. Your father would never approve of it, and there's no way the board would agree."

"Dougal, my friend," came a drawling voice that sounded bored rather than angry. "I dearly hope my father will live for many more years and continue to prop up this project with his investments. But when the time comes, we, the stewards, will have the responsibility of ensuring that Stormhaven is financially stable, and sacrifices will have to be made to achieve that end."

"Not *those* sorts of sacrifices!" Dougal shouted. "That school is the very heart of this community!"

Meghan grabbed Tia's arm, looking down at her as if she had just seen a ghost. "Wyn was right," she whispered. "He wants to turn the castle into a hotel, and he wants to shut the school to do it!"

"Well," they heard Llacheu say with a sigh, "I look forward to hearing what alternatives you can come up with, Dougal, because something has to change."

With a start, the girls realised this comment marked the end of the meeting and that the door would soon open. They did their best to look as though they hadn't been eavesdropping when Llacheu Thunderford appeared in the doorway. Meghan was pretending to be deeply interested in some gulls flying overhead, while Tia was staring intently at her shoes.

Llacheu's small, pale eyes gazed at them suspiciously down his long nose before his thin lips broke into a malevolent smile. "Shouldn't you be at school, girls?" he sneered.

"It's half-term," Meghan said, narrowing her eyes at him.

"Well, it's reassuring to hear that you can cope quite admirably without it." He brushed past them before adding under his breath, "You may need to get used to that."

Meghan looked as though she was about to shout after him. Convinced that any exclamation from her sister was unlikely to be helpful at that moment, Tia hurriedly grabbed Meghan's arm and knocked on the slightly ajar door.

"Come in!" called Professor Dinsmore in a slightly flustered voice.

Tia pushed open the door and they stepped inside.

It seemed as though every available inch of wall space in the tiny room had been crammed with bookshelves, and every available inch of shelf space had been crammed with books. There were at least twenty more books piled up on the desk, each with loose sheets of paper sticking out of it.

The girls were unable to see the small professor behind all the clutter at first, but he came into view as they moved closer. He was sitting back in his chair, staring at nothing in particular and frowning in concentration.

"Ah, girls," he said, his expression transforming into one of pure delight. "I'm so thrilled you were able to come! I'm sorry it's been such a long time coming, but I wanted to express my appreciation for the tremendous smugglers' hoard you discovered a couple of months ago. Those artefacts brought in some much-needed revenue."

"Were they worth a lot, then?" asked Meghan excitedly.

"Er, well, I wouldn't exactly call it a lot," Dougal said rather sheepishly, adding with enthusiasm, "but every little bit helps!" He rummaged in a cupboard under his desk for a moment. "Anyway, it's wonderful to see two promising archaeologists blossoming away at the heart of this special community."

Tia thought it was a bit of a stretch calling what they had done – which basically amounted to crashing through the ceiling of an underground cavern using an ancient standing stone as a battering ram – archaeology, but she didn't say anything. She appreciated the sentiment and Meghan looked thrilled to have been referred to as an archaeologist.

"I asked the chaps in the forge to make you this as a token of my gratitude." As he said this, Dougal pulled out an exact replica of the half-goat, half-fish Roman figurine they had found just a couple of months earlier. "They've done a splendid job. It matches the weight and dimensions of the one you unearthed exactly."

The three of them stared at it, Dougal and Meghan clearly a little awe-struck and Tia simply unsure what to make of the bizarre creature.

"I hope this will inspire you to continue growing in the spirit of Stormhaven," Dougal said as he passed it ceremoniously to Meghan, who handled it like a newborn baby.

"We should put it on the windowsill between our beds," Meghan said as they made their way home.

"It's okay," Tia said hurriedly. "I think it would look good on the bookcase or a shelf on your side of the room."

"*Really?*" Meghan appeared to be quite touched by this suggestion. "Thank you so much!"

Tia had to suppress a smirk as her sister turned to gaze at the goat-fish-baby in her arms with doting eyes. Tia could have sworn her sister was rocking it gently as they walked home.

Chapter Twenty

Confessions

"I got a letter from Nana Ollie today," Mr Trevelyan said at the dinner table after the girls' first day back at school.

"Is she coming soon?" Meghan said at once.

"She said she'll be flying into London on the morning of the third of November," her father explained. "She's going to jump straight on a train and I'll pick her up from the station, so she'll be here when you get home from school that day."

"Brilliant!" exclaimed Meghan.

She placed the goat-fish Dougal had given the sisters (which had been laying in her lap while she ate) on the table so she could stand and take her plate over to the sink.

Mrs Trevelyan puffed out her cheeks and gave a huge sigh at the sight of Meghan's precious treasure. It seemed Tia's mother was as unsure of it as Tia had been. However, Tia found her sister's behaviour highly amusing, and judging by the way Mr Trevelyan chuckled silently as he glanced from his wife to the goat-fish, so did he.

Meghan had taken their trophy into school to show the class that day. Mr Teague had told them the animal was a 'capricorn'; the emblem of the Roman legion stationed in that part of Britain for a couple of hundred years. At the first opportunity, Meghan had raced off to the library to find out more about this legion, and had returned declaring that she had christened the figurine 'Agricola', as that was the name of the legion's most famous general.

Mrs Trevelyan had made it clear that she would only be taking it to school for the one day, but Tia had a feeling that, outside school at least, Meghan and Agricola were likely to be inseparable for some time.

Mrs Trevelyan closed her eyes briefly, as if trying to make herself think of something else. When she opened them again she turned to Tia: "Is there anything you'd especially like to do for your birthday, dear? It's a school day, so we can't go very far, but we could do something in the evening."

Tia didn't know how birthdays usually worked in families. Ms Davidson had done her best to make a fuss of the girls when it was their birthday. There was always a cake and a small gift, but apart from that birthdays were more or less the same as any other day, which had suited Tia.

For Tia, her birthday was a day when she thought of her birth parents more than ever. She assumed at least one of them must be alive, because someone had left her on Ms Davidson's doorstep, but she wondered now whether that might have been Professor Hemyke. She had always tried to slip upstairs as soon as possible on the evening of her birthday, curl up in the window seat of her shared bedroom with the little leather bag in her lap and watch the fireworks. That was the great thing about having a birthday on the fifth of November – there were guaranteed fireworks! It made it feel as though the day was special, and therefore that she was special, without her having to be the centre of attention.

"Do you have fireworks in Stormhaven on the 5th of November?"

"Do we have fireworks?!" exclaimed Meghan. "It's brilliant! Everyone goes up to the top of the hill and we light a bonfire to open the party, and there are burgers and chips and sparklers, and then the fireworks are amazing! Mrs Patel from the Post Office said Bonfire Night falls during Diwali this year, so they're going to have loads of diva candles and lanterns marking the paths up to the top of the hill, too."

"But if you'd rather have a quiet night in we can

do that instead," Mrs Trevelyan added hastily. "Or we could do something completely different."

For a moment Meghan looked horrified at the idea of missing the bonfire and fireworks, but then she seemed to remember that it was Tia's birthday and tried, albeit unsuccessfully, to adopt a neutral expression.

"Could we have a small birthday celebration, just with family?" Tia said after a short pause. "And then go up and join everyone else? I've always enjoyed watching fireworks on my birthday."

"That sounds perfect," said Mrs Trevelyan warmly.

"I reckon Nana Ollie will love that, too," agreed Mr Trevelyan.

"We'll get birthday cake as well as burgers and chips!" grinned Meghan. "Sounds like a brilliant evening to me."

In the few days leading up to Nana Ollie's arrival, Tia worked up the courage to tell her parents how she had removed her silver coins from the burglar's bag before the police arrived. Mr and Mrs Trevelyan listened to her confession in silence, then gazed at each other for a few seconds, as if trying to have a telepathic discussion on how to handle the situation.

"Thank you for telling us, Tia," her mother said at last.

"I doubt this will have affected the police investigation much," Mr Trevelyan said reassuringly, "but we want you to know that you can tell us anything. You never need to keep secrets from us."

Tia gazed from one parent to the other and felt a twinge of guilt. They seemed genuinely hurt that she had kept this information from them… or perhaps it wasn't hurt that was making them look downcast. Perhaps it was *concern* she could see on their faces.

When Tia woke up in need of the bathroom that night she caught a snippet of conversation as she passed her parents' bedroom door.

"Do you really think it's nothing, Tom?"

"I don't know. That bag of silver is easily the most valuable thing in the girls' room, so it could just have been a random burglary. But it does seem strange that she went to the girls' room first. It's almost as if she knew what she was looking for there and only came into our room when she couldn't find the pendant."

Tia heard her father give a half-hearted chuckle. Then he sighed and said: "We're kidding ourselves suggesting this is a coincidence, aren't we?"

Her mother said nothing in response.

Mr Trevelyan continued to think aloud: "So there are

at least two people – possibly working together, possibly not – who want to get their hands on Tia's treasures, and if the same people were behind Geoffrey Hemyke's murder they're prepared to go to pretty desperate lengths."

Tia shivered. It was cold on the landing, but that wasn't the cause of her trembling.

"Oh, Tom!" her mother's voice blubbed. "It's just so unfair on poor Tia. Will she ever have the chance to just be a child? Let's give these people what they want and then maybe they'll leave her alone!"

"You know we can't do that, Gwen. Tia's identity is wrapped up in those treasures of hers. Even if we were able to contact these people, it would be just as unfair on Tia to make her part with them."

She wasn't sure how long she had been doing it, but Tia realised she was clutching her pendant with one hand and had the other arm wrapped around herself. She wanted nothing more than to run into the warmth and light of her parents' room and let them gather her up in their arms, but that would mean admitting she had been eavesdropping and the shame of that felt too great. She resolved to go back to her room silently, then come back out making a bit of noise as she went to the bathroom to signal to her parents that someone was there. But just as she was about to turn, her mother said something that made Tia stop dead.

"Do you still think we were right not to tell her about the letter?"

Letter? Were her parents keeping something from her? Something intricately connected to her story?

"I don't know," her father replied weakly. "It just doesn't seem right to lay the weight of that on her. But then it doesn't seem right to hide anything either."

Tia's head swam, and for a moment she felt as though her trembling might knock her over. She put her hand against the wall to steady herself. Her parents were hiding something from her, and it sounded serious. All of her muscles tensed a little and each breath she took was ever so slightly shallower.

Then her mother's voice made her stop once more. "I just love her so much!"

Tia could hear the tears in her voice.

"I can't believe we've only known her a couple of months," Mrs Trevelyan continued. "It feels like she's always been ours. It's natural that we should want to protect her, isn't it?"

"Of course it is. But she's so brave as well. Maybe she can handle this."

"She shouldn't have to handle it. She's not even ten yet!"

"Gwen, I wish with all my heart that we could somehow have met her years ago. Maybe she need never have become mixed up in this Hemyke business at all! But we can't change the past. And maybe the best way to face the future is to support her instead of simply protecting her."

Tia felt a little less cold than she had a minute earlier. Her muscles weren't as tense and her breath wasn't as shallow.

She was brave and she was loved.

She couldn't explain why, but for some reason that made all the difference in the world. She took in a deep lungful of air, moved her hand from her pendant to the door handle and slowly pushed open the door.

Her parents, who had been sitting on the edge of the bed, leapt to their feet.

"I'm sorry." Tia spoke quickly, racing to get her words out ahead of the rising flood of tears. "I didn't mean to eavesdrop. I was just on my way to the bathroom and I heard you talking and..."

Tia could say no more, and the three of them sat bundled together on the edge of the bed for some time. Nobody spoke until Tia was ready to finish the sentence she had begun.

"I think I am brave enough to know what the letter says," she said softly.

Chapter Twenty-One

The Letter

Mr Trevelyan opened his mouth as if to say something, then shut it again. He opened the drawer in the nearest bedside table, pulled out an envelope and handed it to her.

The letter was addressed to Mr Trevelyan at his castle work address. Tia pulled out a single piece of paper, which looked like a long, hastily scribbled note rather than a letter. It had no sender's address at the top or name at the bottom. The writing was hard to make out in places, but she could just about read it:

Mr Trevelyan, I suggest you drop your enquiries into Geoffrey Hemyke's death. He got on the wrong side of people you don't want to be getting on the wrong side of towards the end of his life, and you wouldn't want to find yourself mixed up in any of it.

He was losing his marbles towards the end, taking some of those legends he loved so much a bit too seriously. I used to ask him how his work was going and he'd say things like: "Bardsey was a diversion. Of course it was!" Then he stopped being able to make eye contact and would just mutter anxiously: "I know the three tests. I know the door. I just need the key."

He began making long journeys and coming back more and more agitated and reclusive. Then he disappeared completely for a few days before they found him dead in his flat, the whole place ransacked.

If you ask me, he wound up owing someone a lot of money; someone who was prepared to do whatever they had to do to get it back. Maybe he was pinning all his hopes on some obscure, long-lost treasure, but whatever he was doing it wasn't rational. He was scared, and maybe the fear drove him mad.

Colleagues went through his notes once the police had finished, just in case there was any scholarly work to be continued, but there was no sign of any serious academic work in those last months.

If you have any sense you'll avoid linking yourself to him in case the same people come after you. As I said, he wasn't involved in any worthwhile research, anyway.

I repeat, drop your enquiries!

It wasn't exactly encouraging, and Tia could see why her parents had been reluctant to share it with her, but it didn't scare her to read it. The writer clearly thought there were some very dangerous people involved in this mystery, and that Professor Hemyke had possibly been insane, but she didn't really know what the rest meant. Tia gazed up at each of her parents in turn, then back down at the note. She didn't even know what question to ask.

"What's Bardsey?" she asked at length, picking out the most obscure word.

"It's an island off the coast of Wales. Some records relating to the legend of the Thirteen Treasures say Merlin took them to the island of Bardsey. Others make no mention of the location."

"So it looks as though Professor Hemyke *was* working on something to do with the Thirteen Treasures of Britain," Tia said excitedly, trying to forget for a moment that there were question marks over his sanity.

"Yes," said Mr Trevelyan, "and it looks as though he thought they were real. The reference to a door might suggest he had found where he thought they were hidden, although he didn't have the right key."

"What about the three tests?" Tia asked, frowning at the letter again.

Her parents shook their heads apologetically, unable to give her an answer.

"I'm sorry we didn't show this to you earlier," her

father said quietly. "It wasn't because we didn't think you were brave enough."

"Your dad only received it yesterday morning," said her mother, "and we don't know who it's from."

"I made so many phone calls to so many people that it could be one of any number of individuals. It sounds as if it's from someone who saw Hemyke quite regularly, though, which means it must be someone in Aberystwyth, either at the university or the library, I imagine. I may be able to find out a bit more when I'm up there for that conference in a couple of months' time."

Tia was exhausted, and she still needed to use the bathroom. Before leaving her parents' bedroom they hugged and kissed her and said that they would keep trying to help her find answers.

So far, Tia thought, *it's been a lot easier to find questions than answers*. Yet, she somehow felt as though she was discovering who she was in the process. That, she had to remind herself, was all she had ever wanted.

As she got back into bed she glanced across at her sister, who was fast asleep with Agricola tucked under one arm. Tia became aware that the fear that had descended on her on the landing had gone, and that she felt safe once again.

She was brave, she was loved and she was safe.

Chapter Twenty-Two

Nana Ollie

"Nana!" Meghan had virtually made Tia run home after school on the 3rd of November, and flung her arms around her grandmother as soon as she caught sight of her in the hallway.

"Goodness, you've grown, Meghan!" the old lady exclaimed.

Tia had imagined Mr Trevelyan's mother as a female version of Grandpa Locryn – the only grandparent she had ever known – but Nana Ollie was entirely different. She was short, slight and moved gracefully. Her face was quite wrinkly, but all the wrinkles were in the right places, giving the impression that she had spent most of her life laughing. She had short grey hair and striking features. It seemed a little strange to Tia to use the word of someone so old, but she couldn't think of one that was more appropriate: she was beautiful.

While she was still being squeezed by Meghan, Nana Ollie winked at Tia and held out a hand towards her. Tia took it and was gently pulled into the embrace.

"Dad said you'd been diving for pirate treasure again," Meghan said breathlessly. "What did you find?"

"Not much treasure, to be honest!" Nana Ollie said with a chuckle. "The wreck we discovered turned out not to be one of Black Bart's pirate ships after all. It was very interesting, though. I've got countless photos of items my team has dredged up in the last year or so if you'd like to see them. I brought them with me because I'm going to speak to a few museum curators while I'm over here to see if I can flog any of our stuff to them."

"Brilliant!" said Meghan gleefully.

"Why don't you go and put your bags in your room, girls?" Mrs Trevelyan suggested. "And then we'll have a look at Nana's photos together."

Five minutes later they were all settled in the living room. Nana Ollie was on the sofa with a granddaughter either side of her. Mr Trevelyan sat on the low wooden stool beside the fireplace so he could get a fire going and Mrs Trevelyan was in the big red armchair opposite him, content just to watch her family enjoying themselves.

"You really should present the photos in a better way if you want museums to take any of this stuff, Mum," said Mr Trevelyan, frowning at the pile of loose photos Nana Ollie had poured out of a large envelope onto the coffee table.

"Yes, you're probably right, Tom," the old lady replied absent-mindedly as she sifted through the pile. "Oh, this is an interesting one, girls!" She held up a large photo of a curved sword. "We found loads of these cutlasses littered across a wreck in the Bahamas last year. The ship was in several pieces and there were dozens of cannonballs lying around."

"Brilliant!" Meghan said again with an awed expression Tia had come to love, and gazed closer at the image.

"What's this?" Tia asked, holding up a photo of what looked like a very grimy and broken old bookcase.

"Ah," said Nana Ollie. Her face seemed to darken a little. "That's a section of the wreck from our most recent dive site."

"The one you thought was one of Black Bart's ships?" Meghan asked.

"Yes. It turned out to be a slave ship that would have transported hundreds, possibly even thousands, of people from Africa to the Caribbean plantations on each voyage. It was quite a harrowing experience being down there and suddenly realising what a barbaric purpose this ship had been used for. There were chains and manacles all over the place." She pointed to a close-up image of some metal cuffs linked together by rusty chains.

"This," she continued, referring back to the photo Tia had found, "was one small section of the hull that had broken off, so we were able to raise it to the surface relatively easily. This is the space a person would have been chained up in for the whole of the long journey across the Atlantic." She highlighted the small rectangular space Tia had at first thought was designed to house a row of books.

The room was quiet for a while, as though the family was observing a moment's silence in remembrance of the unfortunate individual who had been imprisoned in that cramped space, then Nana Ollie sighed. "I'm going to contact Wilberforce House in Hull to see if they want these items. It's a wonderful little museum all about the abolition of slavery. I'm not sure if they'll have room for everything, but I do hope they can take some of it. This story needs to be remembered."

Tia could see tears forming in her grandmother's eyes. Nana Ollie had been staring at the picture for some time and seemed unable to tear her eyes away from it. Tia wanted to spare her the sadness she was obviously experiencing and cheer her up, but somehow that didn't seem the right thing to do just then. Maybe this was the sort of thing her father had been talking about the other night when he said that they should *support* Tia rather than just *protect* her from everything.

She laid a hand on the old lady's arm. "I hope they take it," Tia said. "I think it's really important."

Nana Ollie looked down at Tia, her wrinkly face beaming like the midsummer sun.

The telephone in the hallway rang, and while Mr Trevelyan went to answer it, the others sifted through several more pictures of shipwrecks and sunken treasures.

"That was Locryn, Mum," he said when he returned. "He asked if you're still as good a skittles player as he remembers because we're down a man for our match tonight against the Reluctant Pirate. They've already drafted me in, but now Cedric Howell's shut his hand in his cellar door and we need another replacement urgently."

"Well, I'm rather out of practice," Nana Ollie grinned. "There aren't many pubs with skittle alleys in the Caribbean, but I'm sure it won't take long for the old magic to come back!"

Chapter Twenty-Three

The Jolly Dragon

Soon after dinner the five of them stepped out into a very still, clear and bitingly cold evening to head for the Jolly Dragon, the pub at the end of the road that was home to Grandpa Locryn's skittles team.

It was only a few minutes' walk, but they had all wrapped up well and were grateful to see a roaring fire in the corner of the tiny pub once they got inside. It was so small that only half the bar could be accessed once the skittle alley was folded out. However, the game seemed to attract extra patrons, so the place felt very crowded but extremely jovial. Not only was the landlord, Cedric Howell, unable to play that evening, but his injury meant he had to serve the drinks one-handed. No one seemed to mind the extra time this took, and everyone who had packed themselves into the tiny pub seemed to be having a great time.

Grandpa Locryn waved at the Trevelyans from a table beside the fire and beckoned them over. After greeting him with a kiss on each whiskery cheek, Nana Ollie said she would like to "get her eye in", and the two of them went over to the skittle alley.

Mona Howell, the large, red-faced landlady, came over to collect the pint glass Grandpa Locryn had just finished drinking from. She seemed to laugh almost every time she opened her mouth, but looked like someone who would be able to put even the burliest customer in their place if they stepped out of line, which made Tia wonder whether Cedric Howell had named the pub 'the Jolly Dragon' after his wife.

"Lovely to see your mum again, Tom," she said to Mr Trevelyan. "Is she staying long?"

"We're never quite sure, Mona," he replied.

There was a crashing sound that made everyone at the table look across at the skittle alley, where Nana Ollie was standing with her hands on her hips looking very satisfied with herself.

"She might stay for a while if she can get a couple more skittles matches. How long's Cedric going to be out of action for?"

"The silly old duffer!" Mona laughed heartily. "He'll probably be fine in a week or so. He was moaning like a dying dog earlier, but now the place is full he's giggling and chattering away as if nothing's the matter!"

They all glanced over at the landlord, who seemed to have completely forgotten about his injury.

"Evening, Callum. How are you?" he called out to a customer who had just entered the pub with a wide grin on his face.

"Mr Teague!" Meghan sprang to her feet, her hand shooting up in the air to wave excitedly at the tall, bearded man who had just walked through the door.

He smiled broadly and strode over to their booth, unwinding a green woollen scarf from around his neck as he moved.

"Hello, everybody. Evening, Mona. Busy tonight!"

Mona chuckled a greeting, then bustled back to the bar, collecting empty glasses from a few other tables as she went. Meghan stood up to make room for Mr Teague, who sat between her and Tia just across the table from their parents.

As the adults began talking merrily, Tia glanced around at the happy patrons of the Jolly Dragon. Her gaze lingered on her grandparents, who were discussing the finer points of bowling technique. It would have been impossible not to be swept up by the high spirits that filled the room, but being surrounded by almost all of the most important people in her life had left Tia in a state of bliss. The only thing that could possibly have lifted her mood further would have been the presence of her friend Pasco. *He probably would have felt quite uncomfortable with this many people around him, though,* she thought to herself with a smile.

It seemed incredible to Tia that she hadn't known any of these people for more than three months. Did that matter? Although it had only been three months, she was sure her mother and father knew her better than anyone ever had before. Perhaps that simply meant nobody really knew her. She didn't even really know herself, after all. But so much had happened in the last three months; so much had changed, including Tia herself, that it felt wrong to measure her experience by the passing of time.

"Right."

Mr Trevelyan's voice shook Tia out of her trancelike state.

"I think we're ready to start." He stood up with his glass and walked over to the skittle alley, where the team from the Reluctant Pirate stood waiting, everyone wishing him luck as he went.

Rather than sitting, Meghan had adopted a squatting position beside Mr Teague, as if she were getting ready to pounce. She was staring over at the players with an excited grin on her face, straining to see what was going on. After just two crashes of skittles she left the table to work her way through the crowd in search of a better view. Tia craned her neck but couldn't see much from where she was sitting.

"Tom was telling me you've been seeing a lot of the new nursery teacher," Mrs Trevelyan said to Mr Teague, smirking as she picked up her drink.

Mr Teague suddenly seemed unsure of what to do with his hands, first scratching the back of his neck, then fiddling with his beard and picking up a beer mat, all in quick succession. His cheeks were redder than usual as well, though that might have been due to the cold temperature outside.

He coughed before replying. "Well, she's new to the village, isn't she? Thought it'd be nice if someone showed her round a bit."

Her mother's smirk widened.

Mr Teague glanced sideways at Tia. "What's that you've got there, Tia?" he asked casually.

Tia looked down and was surprised to see her little bag of silver in her hands. She must have distractedly taken it out of her pocket without realising. She considered how to respond for a few seconds. Perhaps because she was feeling so contented that evening and had the security of her mother there, or perhaps because Mr Teague seemed so desperate to change the subject, Tia decided to tell him the truth.

She left out certain details, such as the incident with Mr Silverman, the burglar and the warnings in the letter, but otherwise recounted the full story of how she had been left on the doorstep of Ms Davidson's house with just a few clues, what they had been able to find out about Geoffrey Hemyke so far and the legend of the Thirteen Treasures of Britain.

At first Mr Teague wore an expression of polite curiosity, perhaps just relieved to be talking about something other than his friendship with the new nursery teacher. But his eyes soon widened as he listened, and Tia had a clear sense that he genuinely cared about her story.

"Wow, Tia," he said when she had finished speaking. "That's amazing!"

"Yeah," said Tia, encouraged by his response, "I guess so. I just don't understand how it all connects to me. My dad says he's going to the town where Prof Hemyke lived in a couple of months, and he's going to try to find out a bit more, but it seems like whenever we try to find answers we only end up finding more questions."

"It obviously has something to do with you personally, though," Mr Teague said. "If Hemyke had wanted to leave random clues to the Thirteen Treasures he could have just left the bag on someone's doorstep. Instead, he left it with you. And you must be connected to him in some way because you share his name."

Tia looked at her teacher doubtfully.

"You know," Mr Teague continued, leaning in closer and speaking in a softer voice, "after my first term of teaching at Stormhaven Castle, Ms Morgan took me to one side and explained something to me. I felt like I was a pretty good teacher and that my class had learned loads since I came along. She took me out onto the lawn in front of the school and turned so we could clearly see the name of the school on the side of the building: Stormhaven Castle School of Exploration and Discovery. She said to me: 'Your class has explored and discovered all sorts of things this term, and you should feel very proud of what the children have achieved.'

"I, of course, started to say something modest, but she wasn't finished there. 'My greatest desire, though,' she continued, 'is that while the children are here at my school they'll undertake a greater quest of exploration and discovery; that they'll explore their own identity and discover who they truly are. It's a quest that'll last a lifetime, but it's one that is all about the journey, not the destination.' "

Much like when she had read the letter in her parents' room, Tia had the sense that she was only just grasping what Mr Teague was saying; as if she was only holding on to it with her fingertips. She became aware that she was frowning and hadn't blinked in a while.

Mr Teague took a swig from his glass, then smiled at Tia. "What I mean to say is that exploring this," he pointed to her leather bag and waved a hand around, as if to include everything else that was connected to the treasures, "is important, and don't be discouraged if you keep discovering more questions. You'll still be able to look back and realise you know yourself better than you did before."

Tia glanced up at her mother. The smirk had long vanished from Mrs Trevelyan's face and she was smiling serenely at them both.

"Come on, Dad. I could have knocked more over than that!" Meghan's voice carried over to their table.

They turned their heads towards the skittles match.

"I'm not sure your sister's the most helpful spectator," Mr Teague said to Tia. "Why don't we go over and lend some real support?"

Chapter Twenty-Four

A Birthday Surprise

The 5th of November was a crisp, clear day. As she had back in August on her first morning in Stormhaven, Tia awoke to the sight of her sister's freckly face so close to hers that her bushy hair blocked out almost all the light.

"Happy birthday!" Meghan cried.

"Aaarghhh!" Tia replied, bashing her head with a sense of déjà vu.

Meghan shoved a heavy present gleefully at Tia. Once a large jar of multicoloured jelly beans had been unwrapped, Meghan dragged her sister downstairs to wish their grandmother a happy birthday. Despite Mr and Mrs Trevelyan's protestations, Nana Ollie had insisted on sleeping on the sofa bed in the sitting room rather than taking their room.

Meghan burst into the sitting room, followed a little more sedately by Tia. They found the old lady sitting up in bed, sipping a cup of tea and opening birthday cards. Tia took a seat on the sofa bed while Meghan gave her an energetic birthday greeting.

Tia noticed that each of the envelopes her grandmother had opened bore an exotic-looking foreign stamp, and that no two were the same.

They were soon joined by Mr and Mrs Trevelyan, and after Tia and Nana Ollie had spent twenty minutes opening cards and presents, Mrs Trevelyan pointed out that as it wasn't a public holiday they had all better get moving.

Tia had always found even the smallest amount of extra attention she received on her birthday a little overwhelming. She was being doted on far more than she ever had been at Ms Davidson's house, but having someone else to share the spotlight with was making this one considerably more bearable, and even enjoyable.

Mr Teague seemed to have realised that Tia wouldn't appreciate a lot of fuss, and barely a mention was made of her birthday to the rest of the class.

Roderick Payne, Kezia O'Connor and Tamsyn Wolfe, whose birthdays had occurred earlier in the term, had all brought in cakes and everyone had sung Happy Birthday to them while they blew out the candles. For

Bran's birthday the whole class had gone across the lawn to the forge, where his dad worked most days as an 'experimental archaeologist', researching ancient metal-working techniques. Bran had helped his father demonstrate how to cast a Bronze Age knife, which he had then used to slice up his birthday cake.

Mr Teague had left it until the very end of the day to get the class to sing to Tia, however, and as the others all filed out he pulled her to one side and quietly handed her a small package wrapped in brown paper and string.

"Happy Birthday, Tia," he said. "This is for your quest. You can use it to record all the discoveries you make."

Tia unwrapped it. It was a journal with an emerald green cover and dozens of completely blank pages on which she would be able to write, draw or do whatever she wanted.

"Thank you," she said, smiling up into his beaming, bearded face.

After school, Tia had a pleasant birthday tea with her family. Her mother had made a thick round sponge cake covered in icing, which the family gradually devoured along with glasses of lemonade. Grandpa Locryn and Nana Ollie entertained Tia and Meghan by taking it in turns to recount stories of Mr and Mrs Trevelyan from when they were children.

Meghan had heard many of them before, and requested a couple of specific tales such as the time their mum and Aunt Kensa cut all their hair off to sell to a wigmaker; and the time Uncle James and Uncle George dressed Dad up as a monkey and tried to trade him for the black Labrador belonging to one of the kids down the street.

Pasco arrived in the early evening. Mrs Penrose had asked if the Trevelyans could take him to the fireworks display, as she needed to stay at home with the twins, who disliked the loud bangs and whirrs. Pasco seemed a little uncomfortable at first, as he always did, but he soon found himself contentedly tucking into a piece of birthday cake and enjoying the family stories as much as Meghan and Tia.

It was soon time for everyone to get ready to leave for the fireworks display at the top of the hill. The crisp, clear day had made for a bitingly cold evening, so they wrapped themselves up in thick hats, long scarves and warm gloves.

They walked past the post office to admire the vibrant Rangoli patterns the Patel family had decorated the pavement with, then followed the diva lamps in glass jars that lined the path leading up the hill and out of the village.

The wind wasn't blowing too hard at the top considering it was November, but it was enough to make Tia's face feel numb within five minutes of reaching the summit. She didn't mind, though. In fact, it made the heat of the towering bonfire all the more gratifying.

Once the bonfire had begun to die down, they warmed themselves with burgers and hot dogs. They stood watching it shrink and settle, as if it were a great dragon curling up for a long winter's slumber. Then the adults headed off in search of cocoa and mulled wine before the fireworks began.

Bran slunk over to Tia, Meghan and Pasco looking extremely grumpy after his father appeared in a roped-off section away from the crowds and set about arranging the fireworks, assisted by Bran's two older brothers. Tia understood the reason for his low mood. Bran scowled at his brothers as they began lighting the fireworks, but soon joined the others in gazing up at the multicoloured explosions in the starry sky.

When it was all over, Tia wandered dreamily back down the hill, surrounded by the most important people in the world to her, contentedly sipping what was left of her cocoa.

"Shall we take you straight home, Pasco?" said Mrs Trevelyan once they had all said goodnight to Grandpa Locryn at the end of the path leading up to his tiny cottage beside the chapel.

"Can I just get my bag?" asked Pasco. "I left it in Tia's bedroom."

"Why did you bring a bag and then leave it behind?" said Meghan. "You obviously didn't need anything in it."

"It was to carry Tia's present in," he replied. "Oh,"

he added in a quieter voice, glancing at Tia. "I forgot to give it to you, didn't I?"

It was too dark to tell, but Tia suspected Pasco had turned a bright shade of red at his oversight.

"Not to worry, Pasco," Nana Ollie said cheerily. "You can come in and give Tia her present now. Then we birthday girls will walk you home."

Tia and Pasco went up to the girls' bedroom when they got back to the house, while the others went into the kitchen. Still blushing a little, Pasco pulled a flat square present out of his bag and handed it timidly to Tia, absent-mindedly saying "Sorry" rather than "Happy birthday".

Tia pulled back the wrapping paper to reveal an ancient-looking map in a photo frame. She recognised it at once as a map of Stormhaven Castle and the surrounding area. She took in the village overlooking the bay with Merlin's cave, the castle and the hamlet of Appleketh labelled. The island seemed to be crisscrossed with pathways, and each of the standing stones was also marked.

"My mum's been going through the library archives taking digital images of all the manuscripts, maps and other old documents they've got," Pasco explained. "She said this was one of the oldest maps in the archive, so I thought you might like it. I asked if I could give you the original, but she said it had to stay in the library. She did print me out a really good-quality copy, though."

"Thanks, Pasco," Tia said with a grin, not taking her eyes off the map. "I love it." She stood for a while, staring at every detail as if she were only allowed five minutes with it and needed to commit it all to memory. "Does your mum know how old it is?" she asked, sitting down on her bed.

"She reckons about four or five hundred years."

"Maybe we could go and explore the island with it this weekend," she said excitedly, looking up from the map for the first time. "It shows footpaths all over the island that I'm pretty sure aren't all there any more. I've no idea what half of these markings mean, but I'd love to find out what's out there. Oh no!"

While she was talking, Tia had absent-mindedly been trying to wriggle her little leather bag out of the back pocket of her jeans with one hand as the silver coins were rather uncomfortable to sit on. As she finally wrenched the pouch free, the pieces inside had gone flying across the room through a tear in the seam. She had been carrying it around constantly since the attempted burglary, and all the extra handling and shoving it in and out of pockets had finally become too much for the old pouch.

Pasco got down on his hands and knees to help Tia

locate some of the coins, which had slipped down beside the chest of drawers. They soon recovered all twelve and piled them up in the middle of the floor. Tia examined the pouch, putting a small hand inside and poking a finger out through the tear.

"I guess this bag is pretty old," she said, frowning at her wiggling finger. "I should probably get a new one. But this is the bag all the pieces were in when they were first left with me. It's like one of the treasures itself, though not quite as old."

"We can probably fix it," Pasco said, holding out a hand to inspect the bag.

Tia handed it to him, looking hopeful.

"I reckon we might be able to sew up the seam if we turn it inside out," he continued.

"Do you know how to sew?" Tia asked doubtfully.

"Well, no," Pasco admitted sheepishly. "My mum can, though, and I'm sure she'd do it for you. Look." He turned the bag inside out and indicated where it could be sewn up. "We could just staple it for now, if you want."

Tia decided this was a good idea. It felt wrong to store the pieces of silver in anything else, even just temporarily until Mrs Penrose could repair the bag.

"Okay," she said, smiling at Pasco.

She walked over to a small drawer in her sister's bedside table and rummaged around for a stapler. Meghan kept several useful tools in there and many others that were not so useful.

"Tia," Pasco said quietly while Tia's back was turned to him. "When you gave the coins to your parents to look at, did you give them this bag, too?"

"Hmm?" Tia said distractedly. It was proving harder than she had expected to locate anything specific among all the junk in Meghan's drawer.

"When your dad looked at the silver pieces," Pasco repeated, still not quite in his usual voice, "did he also see this bag?"

"Er, no." She paused her search, realising how strange it was that she hadn't insisted on her father keeping the coins in their bag. But handing them over in the first place had been so strange anyway that this hadn't occurred to her at the time. Besides, it had been reassuring to at least keep hold of the bag while she was without the treasures it had always held.

She was jolted out of her thoughts by the sight of the stapler she had been searching for. "Ah, here it is!" She straightened up and turned around, checking to see whether there were any staples in it. She tutted and sighed. "It's empty." She looked up at Pasco and was a little startled by his appearance.

His face had turned pale and he was staring at her wide-eyed, holding the leather pouch in one outstretched hand. "Look!" he said, extending it a little further towards her.

Tia took a step closer and hesitantly lowered her eyes

from her friend's face to the pouch in his hand. She gasped. The stapler slid from her hand and landed on the floor with a thud. With two hands, and as gently as if it were a sleeping kitten, she picked up the leather bag she had thought she knew so well. She blinked and looked again to make sure that what she thought she had seen was really there.

It was.

Written on the inside of the bag, in what looked like faded red pen, was a string of numbers, letters and symbols:

53°58'56"N 0°30'27"W

Tia's mouth felt dry and her head was spinning. It seemed incredible to her that in all the years she had kept this little bag hidden away under her mattress she had never once turned it inside out. But then why would she? Still, Tia couldn't quite believe she was gazing at something she had never seen before, yet was a part of something she knew so well.

Her first thought was that Pasco had just written it there himself, but the lettering clearly wasn't fresh. *Perhaps the burglar wrote it*, she mused. But it was so old and faded it would have been hard to read if they hadn't happened to be standing beneath the bedroom light. It had obviously been hidden away there for several years. For Tia it was like suddenly discovering that a life-long friend was really an escaped criminal living under a false name.

Once the initial shock had subsided a little, she was able to move beyond its mere existence to consider what the writing actually meant. She felt the familiar sensation of a fresh discovery being swiftly followed by a stampede of yet more questions.

At least three minutes had passed in complete silence since the thud of the stapler hitting the floor, and when Tia eventually spoke it was little more than a whisper.

"What does it mean?" She was talking more to herself than to Pasco, so it startled her when he answered.

"I think I might know," he said simply.

Chapter Twenty-Five

What Pasco Knew

On the Friday of the following week, Tia sat gazing out of the classroom window at the end of a long school day. She felt sick.

The previous week she had been so desperate for this weekend to come, but now that it had arrived her stomach was heavy with dread. What on earth had made her think anything good could come of this? Surely she should have realised by now that every answer just led to more questions.

Her gaze shifted from the window to the book she was clutching in her hands: the journal Mr Teague had given her. What did he say Ms Morgan had told him? Something about self-discovery being a quest that takes a lifetime but it being about the journey, not the destination.

The battle between the hope in her heart and the dread in her stomach couldn't be resolved. She had to go, Tia knew that, because she knew she couldn't live without following the trail. Regardless of what the weekend had in store for her – answers, more questions, or nothing at all – she had no choice but to go. Whatever happened, she would return on Sunday to a family and a home where she was safe and loved. That much she could be sure of, and it gave her courage.

She opened the journal, which she had used to write notes on everything she had worked out so far. The first three pages were taken up with sketches she had made of her pendant, the pieces of silver and the leather pouch, including an illustration of it inside out to show the faded writing. The fourth page was all about Geoffrey Hemyke:

> Professor Geoffrey Hemyke, University of Wales
>
> - Expert in myths and legends of ancient Britain
> - Died in mysterious circumstances at his home in Aberystwyth
>
> Weird things people heard him say just before he died:
>
> "I know the three tests. I know the door. I just need the key."

"Bardsey* was a diversion, of course it was!"

*Bardsey Island: where the legend says Merlin hid the Thirteen Treasures

The fifth, sixth and seventh pages contained the full list of the Thirteen Treasures of Britain, including the names of people they were said to belong to and descriptions of the objects' magical properties. Tia almost knew the list off by heart, and had done for weeks, but she still found it hard to remember the strange-sounding names of all the people from whom Merlin had acquired them.

On the eighth page of the journal was her most recent discovery:

53°58'56"N 0°30'27"W
St Mary's Church, Kirkburn, East Yorkshire

Tia was shaken from her reverie by the sound of her classmates getting to their feet and heading for the door. Mr Teague had obviously dismissed them for the weekend.

"I'm just popping to the library to say goodbye to Mum." Pasco seemed to be talking to her. "I'll see you in the courtyard," he added as he left the classroom.

Pasco had immediately recognised the writing on the inside of the pouch as longitude and latitude co-ordinates. They had descended the stairs that evening and entered the kitchen with some trepidation. After showing everyone their discovery, Mr Trevelyan had fetched his laptop and typed in the co-ordinates. Tia remembered how quickly her heart had been beating as the map zoomed in closer and closer, eventually coming to rest on an aerial photograph of a small village church in East Yorkshire.

Even Meghan had been shocked into silence at this discovery for a few seconds, though it hadn't taken long for her to begin making plans for them all to jump in the car and immediately set off for Yorkshire. She was convinced the Thirteen Treasures must be hidden in a churchyard tomb and seemed to think they should all head over there without delay.

Once Mr Trevelyan had explained just how long it would take to drive to the village, and Mrs Trevelyan had firmly stated that no one would be missing any school for this, Meghan accepted that it would at least have to wait for the weekend. Neither of the girls had slept much that night. Meghan had eventually stopped talking long enough to fall asleep at about one o'clock. Tia, on the other hand, wasn't sure she had slept a wink.

At breakfast the next morning, Nana Ollie had said she would take them up to Yorkshire the following weekend. She had arranged to meet with someone from the Wilberforce House Museum in Hull that Saturday, and Kirkburn wasn't far from there. If they left straight after school, they could arrive late on the Friday and come back on the Sunday.

While her grandmother and father had sat at the table with them, sharing this plan, Mrs Trevelyan had stood at the sink with her arms folded, biting her bottom lip and looking worried. Tia wondered how long the adults had stayed up working out what to do, and how reluctantly Mrs Trevelyan had agreed to it.

Since then, Tia had become increasingly apprehensive about the trip but was determined to go. She would have liked her parents to come with her, but they needed to leave as soon as school ended and it was too short notice for her father to get the afternoon off work. Her mother had a deadline for a paper the following Monday and needed to get through a mound of work over the weekend.

Tia had immediately asked if Pasco could go with them. If she couldn't have her parents there, Pasco would be the next best person to help her decipher any further clues they might find. Nana Ollie had immediately approved, providing his mother allowed it, and at Pasco's insistence Mrs Penrose had agreed.

In contrast to Tia's misgivings, Meghan had become increasingly excited about the trip, first calling it a treasure hunt and then simply referring to it as 'The Quest'. Every night for the past week, once the girls were in bed with the lights off, Meghan had recounted her latest idea as to what they would find in Kirkburn.

The theory she had settled on was that they would probably find a tombstone with the sort of slot found on vending machines, into which Tia would have to pay the twelve silver coins. A stone would then slide away to reveal a staircase leading down to an underground chamber that housed the Thirteen Treasures. She figured it would probably have a locked door, and that Tia's pendant would be the key for it.

Tia left the classroom in a daze. She found herself in the courtyard approaching the Trevelyan family's little purple car with no recollection of leaving the keep or crossing the causeway. Meghan was standing off to the side next to one of the outbuildings talking to three of the university students who were working at Stormhaven Castle for the term. Tia had no doubt as to what her sister was talking to them about and didn't fancy joining in the conversation, so she continued towards the car where her parents and Grandpa Locryn were helping Nana Ollie load bags into the boot.

"Now, you take care," her mother said, grabbing hold of Tia as soon as she saw her and squeezing her tightly, "and stay close to your nana at all times."

"We're only going for two nights." Tia tried her best to sound casual but made no attempt to escape the embrace.

"It might only be for two nights," Grandpa Locryn said warmly, coming over to bid her farewell, "but that's a long time for a mother." He knelt down and hugged her, then stood up and put an arm round Mrs Trevelyan. "They'll be fine, Gwen."

Just then, Pasco appeared in the courtyard, hurried over to the car and deposited his bag in the boot. He smiled weakly at them all. He was proud of the discovery he had made, without which the expedition would not have been happening, and excited about the trip, but Tia knew he was apprehensive about being away from home for a whole weekend.

"Right," said Mr Trevelyan, shutting the car boot, "I think you're all set. Tia, make sure Nana doesn't drive too fast, and that she stops for a break after two hours."

He smirked as he said this, looking sideways at Nana Ollie, who tutted and raised her eyebrows. Tia managed a half-hearted chuckle.

Mr Trevelyan called Meghan away from the students, who hurried away as soon as they were free, looking relieved. Final goodbyes were said, and Tia and Pasco climbed into the back seat, Meghan having already claimed the front seat. With the others waving them off, Nana Ollie drove out of the castle courtyard and onto the road that led through Appleketh.

Meghan and Nana Ollie chatted most of the way, while Tia and Pasco preferred to gaze thoughtfully out of their windows. As instructed, they stopped after a couple of hours and had some dinner. It was quite dark and had started to rain when they set off again. By the time they reached their destination, everyone was ready for bed.

They were staying in one of the private rooms in a youth hostel between Kirkburn and Hull so they could easily reach both places the following day. The room was simple but comfortable, containing two sets of bunk beds. Nana Ollie climbed onto one top bunk and Meghan onto the other, both falling asleep within seconds. After clambering into their respective bottom bunks, Tia and Pasco lay awake for a while.

"How do you feel?" Pasco whispered in the dark.

"Not sure," Tia answered. "I think I mostly just feel sick." She slipped one hand under her pillow to touch the patched-up leather pouch holding the twelve silver coins, one finger of her other hand tracing the cross-shaped pattern on the pendant around her neck. "I'm scared and excited, but I don't want to get my hopes up. It might all come to nothing."

"That's how I feel, too," Pasco said. "I mean, I'm sure I don't feel it as strongly as you do," he added. "I'm just glad I can be here with you for all this," he said after a pause.

"So am I." Tia felt a tear run silently down her cheek but wasn't sure why. It felt good to let something out, though. She squeezed her eyes shut, trying to wring out more tears and press as much feeling as she could into each drop without making a sound.

Chapter Twenty-Six

X Marks the Spot

They left early the next morning, each of them carrying a few essential supplies in their backpacks. They stopped for breakfast at a café in the market town before heading off to Hull for Nana Ollie's meeting at Wilberforce House, where she was due to discuss her slave-ship findings. Nana Ollie apologised to Tia that she hadn't been able to rearrange her meeting for later in the day so they could go to Kirkburn first.

Tia appreciated the thought, but it didn't help her feel any less sick. It was hard for her to focus on anything that morning. She vaguely remembered passing two short, square-shouldered men as they left the youth hostel, but hadn't noticed the woman who had placed her breakfast in front of her at the café at all. She had barely eaten a thing and felt as though she got out of the car in Hull just a few seconds after getting in. She drifted around the museum with Meghan and Pasco while Nana Ollie was at her meeting, and when that was over she gave a silent nod in agreement with her grandmother's statement: "One can't possibly come to Hull and not have fish and chips for lunch." She was unable to eat a single chip, however.

She got back in the car with the others once they had finished eating, and after a sickening journey that had nothing to do with the motion of the vehicle they pulled up in front of the church in Kirkburn. As she passed through the wooden gate to the churchyard, Tia clutched the pendant dangling from her neck with one hand and placed her other on the bulge in her pocket where the bag of silver lay.

"Okay, Tia, where…" Nana Ollie looked as though she was about to ask Tia where she wanted to go first, but on seeing how pale she looked, decided it might be better to make a suggestion than ask a question. "Let's have a look inside first, shall we?" she said hastily. "Loads of churches are open during the day. We'll need to be quiet, though." She eyed Meghan meaningfully as she said this. "Others may want to use the church to pray."

It was a grey, overcast day, dry but without a breath of wind. Having been in a daze all day, and not being able to see the sun, Tia had no idea what time of day it was. It felt like night might be drawing in, but this was the sort of day when twilight seemed to linger from dawn until dusk; the sort of autumnal English day that never quite finds the energy to fully wake.

As they walked down the path, Tia glanced at the graveyard to her left and right. She doubted Meghan's theory about finding a grave with a coin slot, but she did think they were more likely to find clues outside than inside; a tombstone bearing the name of one of those mentioned in the legend of the Thirteen Treasures, perhaps.

Tia had brought her journal with her so she could check the names, but the tombstones looked rather foreboding at the moment. She decided a little time within the shelter of the church building might give her churning stomach a chance to settle before she began tackling the imposing blocks of cold stone outside.

The large wooden door was unlocked, as Nana Ollie had thought it might be, but there was no one inside. There was a peaceful ambience that even Meghan seemed to appreciate, though she couldn't remain completely silent. "I'm telling you, the entrance to the secret chamber is bound to be in the graveyard," she said in a hushed voice. "Ooh! Or maybe up there!"

She had spotted an extremely narrow stone staircase leading up into the tower. Nana Ollie placed a gentle hand on her granddaughter's shoulder to stop her leaping up the first few steps.

"Let's have a look around down here first," she said with a smile. "Besides, it would have to be a pretty small secret chamber to be hidden up there. And one of the treasures is a chariot, isn't it? Merlin might have been a magician, but even he would have struggled to get a chariot up those steps!"

Pasco and Tia laughed. It felt good to laugh, as though it helped to force out some of whatever was making Tia feel queasy. Meghan reluctantly moved away from the steps, casting a longing look back over her shoulder to the point where the stone staircase disappeared into the ceiling.

There was a row of wooden pews on either side of the aisle that led through an archway and up a couple of steps to an altar at the far end. There seemed to be archways everywhere Tia looked; around carvings and paintings on the walls, and over several doorways and windows. At the nearest end of the aisle was a large round pedestal carved out of solid stone. This was the font, where children were christened to welcome them into the community of the church.

The four of them wandered around individually, looking at various painted images and carvings in the stonework.

Tia wasn't able to take in much of what she was looking at. She just wanted to use the time to settle her nerves. It was tranquil in the church and she could feel a sense of calmness coming over her.

"Can we have a look outside now?" she asked after a while.

Nana Ollie smiled and nodded. Addressing the three of them together, she said: "Now, I want you to remember that people are buried out there, so we need to have some respect as we walk around their graves. Try not to step on the graves themselves, and let's move quietly rather than running around and shouting to one another."

They all nodded in agreement and moved towards the door.

The churchyard that had seemed quite eerie on the way in somehow felt different now. The paleness of the green grass and grey stone in the wintry half-light cast a spell of serenity over Tia, in stark contrast to the spell of dread they had cast earlier. The air was as cool and still as it had been previously, but it felt a little fresher and cleaner; less cold and biting. She breathed in two deep lungfuls of that air, and the restlessness that had been lingering in her stomach finally ceased altogether.

Meghan had already set off excitedly, weaving through the graves, though she was clearly trying to be as respectful as possible. Nana Ollie said she would take a look around the outside walls while Tia and Pasco stuck together and began examining the gravestones.

Many of them were extremely old and worn, and proved almost impossible to read. Others were more recent but had very normal-sounding names written on them; nothing close to the obscure names from the legend of the Thirteen Treasures. At one point Tia thought she had found an old stone bearing the worn remains of the letters "Hem" and stared long and hard at it in an attempt to make the rest of the scratchings form the letters "yke", but Pasco hesitantly pointed out that the "m" was actually "re" and that it probably said "here lies", followed by someone's name. After half an hour of looking, Tia was beginning to feel disheartened. She suggested that they go back inside.

"I'll stay out here for a bit longer with Meghan," Nana Ollie said, smiling sympathetically and patting Tia on the shoulder. "She's round the back at the moment and seems to be doing quite a thorough inspection."

Perhaps there's another piece of information we're missing, Tia thought to herself as she and Pasco walked back inside the church. *Maybe Mr Trevelyan will be able to find something out while he's in Aberystwyth in the new year, and then we'll have an idea of what we should be looking for in this place.*

Or perhaps Professor Hemyke was just crazy.

She glanced over to Pasco, who was standing in the aisle looking up at some stone carvings. She really appreciated his calm, quiet presence as well as her sister's energy and enthusiasm, and thought how Nana Ollie must really care to have offered to drive the three of them up north and look after them for an entire weekend. She thought of her parents, of her grandfather and of Stormhaven Castle, and all of a sudden the disappointment of not finding anything there seemed to matter less.

As Tia looked away from Pasco, her eyes fell on the stone font at the opposite end of the church to the altar. She hadn't looked closely at it earlier, so she walked over to peer at the carvings.

It was crammed with what looked like people and animals chiselled out of a solid piece of stone. They were roughly carved and almost looked like children's drawings embossed onto the stone. It seemed a little out of place among the sophisticated paintings on the church's wooden panelling and the carvings Pasco was still gazing up at, which looked as though much more care had been taken over them.

Tia slowly circled the stone, trying to work out what the carvings were supposed to depict. First she examined the upper row of figures, many of which were holding keys, staffs and other items. Then she looked down at the lower row, which appeared to show different sorts of animals. It was then that she saw something which made her heart freeze and leap up into her throat.

There, enclosed in a square stone frame, between what looked like a snake that had tied itself in a knot and a fox tied to the leg of a dwarf, was a symbol in the shape of an X.

A symbol that Tia knew extremely well.

Chapter Twenty-Seven

The Four Bridges

"Pasco…"

Tia's mouth had dried up and her friend's name came out as a hoarse whisper that he had no hope of hearing. She knelt down to look at the symbol, removing the pendant from around her neck as she did so. The X-shape was formed by two squashed, intertwining ovals just like the one on her pendant. Solomon's knot… that was what her father had called it. Tia remembered him saying it was quite a common symbol.

Could this just be a coincidence?

Remembering Meghan's fanciful theory of a treasure chamber, Tia held the pendant up against the stone with trembling fingers to see if it would somehow click into place, but it was a little too large to fit inside the hole in the middle of the symbol and too small to sit comfortably on top of it. She traced the outline of the shape on the stone with her finger, and as she did so her hand seemed to stop shaking.

"Pasco," she said again, a little more audibly this time.

Pasco turned, his eyes widening at the expression on her face.

"Have you found something?" he said, hurrying down the aisle towards her.

"Maybe," she answered, her voice quivering slightly. Tia stopped tracing the symbol with her finger and placed the palm of her hand over it. The coldness of the stone became warm under her hand. "Look at – "

Tia gasped and started scrambling backwards away from the font just as Pasco reached her. The great stone pedestal was slowly sliding away from them to reveal a dark hole in the floor just large enough for a person to slip through. It moved with a scraping rumble that made Tia's bones tremble.

When it finally stopped, the church seemed to echo with the sound of Pasco's breathless panting and her own heart thumping against her ribcage. The two friends stared at the hole and then at each other, with a look that said: *Did you just see what I saw?*

Tia tentatively crawled forward and peered into the blackness.

"I think it's a tunnel," she said, leaning down as far as she dared. Her voice had no echo, as if all sides of the tunnel were made of soft earth rather than a hard substance.

As her eyes adjusted to the gloom, she thought she saw a pale glow coming from somewhere further down the tunnel and around a bend. "There's a light down there!"

Pasco edged towards the brim of the pit, creeping along the floor of the church. He gulped, then peered down his nose into the tunnel, not wanting to incline his body for fear of tumbling in. "I can't see a light."

"It's very faint. You need to lean in a bit," she said with slight exasperation, looking up at him, "so your eyes can adjust to the dark."

She gave him a light tug on the sleeve, which she intended to be encouraging. However, Tia's growing excitement and Pasco's growing nervousness meant that this tug was enough to throw him off balance. He snatched at her in an attempt to steady himself, but she was already leaning a long way over and tipped forward herself. Tia was just able to grip on to the stony edge of the church floor, but having already disappeared into the blackness, Pasco made one last frantic grab for anything that might save him and caught hold of Tia's backpack, sucking her into the pit with him.

After a lot of bumping, rolling and moaning, the two of them came to rest on a soft soil floor. Their heavy breath was the only sound, somewhat muffled by the spongy earthen walls of the tunnel. The absence of any echo made the space seem cramped, as if they had just been buried alive.

"Are you okay?" Tia panted.

Pasco whimpered in response, but it was a whimper of alarm, not pain.

The pair had tumbled down a steep earthy incline rather than falling down a vertical drop, so thankfully they weren't hurt. Tia could feel the soil on her hands and clothes, and could taste it in her mouth where she had landed face first in the dirt.

She could see a circle of light at the top of the slope where they had entered the tunnel. It wasn't a great distance away, but Tia could see at a glance that it would be too far to reach, even if she stood on Pasco's shoulders, and the slope was too soft and steep to scramble up.

Tia turned back in the other direction and saw the pale glow she had seen from above once again, though it was still too faint to decide even what colour it was. She stood up slowly at first to avoid hitting her head on a ceiling, but when she stretched up with her hands she was only just able to reach the soil above. This also felt soft, and for a moment she wondered whether the tunnel might cave in on them. She shook the thought off. It was time to be brave again. She stretched her hands out to the sides and was unable to touch both walls of the passageway at the same time.

"It's all right, Pasco."

Pasco made a high-pitched noise, as if to say that the situation was anything but 'all right'.

"The tunnel's quite big," she said. "You can stand up, and there's room enough for us to walk side by side."

There was a scrabbling sound, then Tia felt Pasco standing beside her.

"Can you see the light now?" she asked. "Let's go and see what's down there."

She had expected him to protest at this and demand that they stay where they were and wait for Nana Ollie and Meghan to come back inside the church and see what had happened, but Pasco seemed incapable of speech and simply clung to her arm as they set off. Part of her knew that staying put was probably the most sensible thing to do, but the adrenaline of this incredible discovery, and the desire to explore more, was so strong she felt compelled to go further.

They walked forward slowly. At first it became even darker in the tunnel as they moved away from the light spilling down from the tunnel entrance, but it soon began to grow ever so slightly lighter as they moved forward. It was hard to tell whether that was because they were getting closer to the source of the glow or because their eyes were becoming accustomed to the dark.

It was impossible to know how far they had gone or how much time had passed. It felt as though they were going straight and slightly downwards, but it was hard to be sure of that either.

On they went in silence. By this point they could clearly make out the curved roof of the tunnel and the flat floor, though it was all the colour of dark brown earth, without a single rock or tree root poking out. Then they began to see something different forming in the gloom ahead of them. They couldn't make anything out clearly, but it seemed as though they were coming to the end of the dark tunnel and the start of something else entirely.

The earthen floor of the tunnel abruptly turned to flagstones, and they found themselves at the foot of a stone spiral staircase just like those in the turrets of Stormhaven Castle. The light there was much stronger. A silvery-blue light like the glow of a full moon on a cloudless night fell down on the stones from somewhere up the stairs, making them sparkle and glisten.

Tia turned to face Pasco with an enquiring look. He seemed calmer now, but there were signs of internal struggle in his eyes. Curiosity seemed to win out over fear and he nodded. It was too narrow to go up side by side, as they had as they walked through the tunnel, so Tia went ahead, with Pasco following closely behind.

After spiralling round once, small narrow windows began to appear high up on the wall. The strange blue light was pouring in through the glass, illuminating their steps. Then, after another couple of turns, they emerged onto the roof of the turret. They looked around and gasped.

They were standing at the top of a stone tower in the middle of an enormous underground chamber. Four narrow stone bridges sprouted out from the top of the tower in different directions, each leading to an archway in the wall of the cavern. All around them were flaming torches in sconces, each burning with the silvery blue light they had seen from down below. In the middle of the roof of the tower they were standing on was a stone pedestal topped with gold.

"Which way now, do you think?" Tia asked.

"No idea," Pasco said softly.

It was the first time he had spoken since they had fallen into the hole.

Was that two minutes or two hours ago? Tia wondered.

"Maybe we should just have a peep through the archways to see if we can see where they lead," she suggested, moving towards the nearest bridge.

The moment she placed her foot on the bridge, the stones beneath it crumbled.

Chapter Twenty-Eight

The First Test

Tia fell and spun in the air, scrabbling for a handhold to stop herself plummeting to the floor of the cavern along with the stone bridge. The first stone she reached for came away in her hand, showering her with shards of rock and forcing her to hold her breath and close her eyes as the dust fell. The thunderous sound of enormous lumps of stone scraping against each other and crashing to the floor echoed around the cavern, and Tia felt completely disorientated. She could feel herself falling, her arms flailing in the hope of blindly catching hold of something.

Anything.

She found nothing.

But then something caught hold of her.

Pasco threw himself forward without thinking and caught hold of Tia's arm just as she disappeared over the edge. She dangled there while the bone-crunching sound of stone hitting stone filled the cavern.

As the rumbling died down, Tia could feel Pasco's sweaty hand losing its grip on hers. She opened her eyes, which had been scrunched shut against the billowing clouds of debris that had filled the air, and met Pasco's stricken gaze.

She was slipping through his fingers.

With a grunt of effort, Pasco lunged for Tia with his other hand and grabbed hold of her wrist just as his first hand lost its grip.

Once it was quiet again, Pasco took a deep breath and hauled her up to safety. The two of them lay on their backs for some time, sucking as much air into their lungs as possible in an attempt to still their thumping hearts. They were both caked in dust.

"Thanks," Tia said after a while.

"No problem," panted Pasco, still looking shocked.

"Well, now we've only got three options," Tia said, getting to her feet and brushing herself down.

"I can see a fourth," said Pasco, eying the way down to the spiral staircase as he wiped his glasses with a scarf from his backpack.

"How on earth are we supposed to know which bridge is the right way to go?" said Tia, ignoring the option of going back. "I'd prefer not to do *that* again," she added, nodding in the direction of the collapsed bridge.

When Pasco didn't respond, she turned around to look at him. He was frowning thoughtfully at the stone pedestal. Tia looked at it more closely and saw that the top wasn't entirely gold, as she had thought at first glance. A large square of gold had been set into its surface; a square that had been divided into a grid of smaller squares.

"A chessboard," Tia whispered.

"A *gwyddbwyll*." Pasco pronounced the word as 'gwid-bill', as he hadn't yet mastered the tricky Welsh sounds. He looked up at her and smiled. "Look, it's a seven-by-seven grid, just like Brandubh."

Tia pulled her journal out of her bag and riffled through the pages until she came to her list of the Thirteen Treasures of Britain.

"The Gwyddbwyll of Gwenddolau," she read aloud, purposely using the Welsh word instead of chessboard, though she still couldn't quite pronounce it correctly either. "If the pieces were set, they would play by themselves."

"But where are the pieces?" Pasco looked down at the floor around him, then inspected the pedestal itself, hoping to discover some sort of secret compartment.

Tia turned back to her journal and read the next sentence. "The board was of gold, and the men of silver." She pulled the leather bag of silver pieces out of her pocket and weighed it thoughtfully in her hand.

Pasco looked up at the clinking metal sound and his eyes widened. "Of course!"

Tia handed him the leather bag and stared at the golden board as Pasco carefully emptied the contents onto it.

"Well, the pieces with circles on them must be the attackers, because there are eight of them," he said, "and the ones with the crosses are the king's men, but where's the…" Pasco stopped and looked up at Tia, who was already unthreading her pendant from its chain. "… King," he finished, taking the thirteenth piece from her hand.

As Pasco began arranging the pieces on the board, Tia thought of all the bizarre things that had happened so far: the font sliding away; the tunnel it had revealed; this incredible chamber; the way the bridge had crumbled beneath her feet. Yet finally discovering the purpose of the treasures she had known for so long was the most surreal thing. The sight of Pasco arranging her thirteen treasures on the golden Chessboard of Gwenddolau was making the hairs on the back of her neck stand on end more than any of those earlier experiences.

"There," Pasco said. He backed away from the pedestal, eying the silver pieces nervously.

Nothing happened.

"Maybe it was a bit silly to expect them to start

moving on their own," Tia said, her voice heavy with disappointment.

"Hmm. Or maybe this isn't the way the pieces were set in a game of gwyddbwyll." Pasco adjusted his glasses and started rearranging the pieces.

Tia looked back at the journal in her hands. She flicked to the page about Geoffrey Hemyke.

I know the three tests. I know the door. I just need the key.

They too had found the door and even managed to open it, although Tia still wasn't sure how. She had thought the pendant was the key, but it hadn't really fitted properly and now seemed to have some other purpose. Presumably, this was the first test.

As she wondered what the other two tests might be, Pasco let out a loud gasp and jumped back from the pedestal, staring at the golden board. He must have happened upon the correct arrangement because the silver pieces were moving around completely on their own.

The only noise in the chamber was the soft scraping sound made by each piece as it moved in turn. Tia silently slipped the journal back into her bag and edged over to Pasco, neither taking their eyes off the game being played by invisible phantoms.

"Do you think there'll be some sign telling us which way to go once the game's finished?" Tia whispered.

"The king has to get to a corner to escape," Pasco

answered, still staring at the ghostly game, "and each corner's pointing to one of the bridges. I reckon whichever corner he gets to will show the direction we're supposed to take."

Tia glanced up from the board at the four bridges and saw that each golden corner of the square board did indeed seem to point straight along a bridge and through an archway. Not for the first time, she marvelled at the way Pasco's brain worked. Then a slightly uncomfortable thought occurred to her.

"What if it points to the bridge that collapsed?" Tia felt her stomach drop as she uttered the words. She tried to find something light-hearted to say. "Will we have to jump?"

Pasco looked at her and blinked, unsure whether she was joking or not. While they were looking at one another, the scraping sound stopped and the chamber fell silent once more. Their gaze snapped down to the board to see where the king had ended up. He was sitting in the corner square furthest away from them, indicating a bridge that was still intact.

They sighed with relief and were about to step around the pedestal when the chamber suddenly rang out with a great cracking sound, followed by a rumble. Then there was a crashing of stone on stone once more as the other two bridges crumbled like the first.

The two friends stood motionless until the crashing faded into an echo, then ceased altogether. Without saying a word, they walked around the pedestal and headed for the one remaining bridge, which corresponded with the corner square the king was standing on.

Tia stopped as they passed the golden board. She turned and gathered the silver pieces back into her bag. If there were two more tests to come they might need them again; they had no other clues, after all. And even if they had served their purpose, she couldn't bear to leave them behind after all these years.

They hurried across the bridge and through the archway to find themselves in another earthen tunnel. This one was wider, however, and there were silvery-blue torches flickering in sconces attached to the walls, as there had been in the cavern.

As they walked through the tunnel they discussed what the next two tests might be, and Tia began to think they might really find a treasure chamber at the end of the trail. Perhaps there would also be a clue as to how on earth she was connected to all of this. At the very least, the treasure trove would hopefully be valuable enough to keep Stormhaven out of Llacheu Thunderford's money-grabbing clutches.

They turned a corner in the passageway and halted abruptly. A few paces ahead, the tunnel opened out into another chamber. This one was much smaller than the first and its walls were made of earth rather than stone. From where they stood, Tia and Pasco could see a large table in the middle of the chamber, sitting upon which was an ornately decorated basket, a drinking horn, a clay pot and dish, and a knife. Behind it, hanging in a niche in the chamber wall, was a cauldron about the size of a wastepaper basket. To one side they could just make out the edge of a great wooden wheel and the back end of a wooden chariot.

"This is it?" said Tia, thrilled, if a little puzzled. "Already? What about the other two tasks?"

"I don't know," Pasco replied as they slowly moved forward. "Maybe Hemyke was wrong."

The hopefulness in Pasco's voice vanished with a parting squeak as something made them stop dead in their tracks, their hearts leaping up into their throats once again. It was the sound of a man's voice; not loud, but sharp and as strong as steel.

"Halt! Don't take another step!"

Chapter Twenty-Nine

The Second Test

A tall, broad, powerfully built man moved out of the shadows and stood directly in front of Tia and Pasco. He wore a dark green tunic with three bloodstained holes in it, a leather belt around his waist, and a brown cloak over his shoulders, fastened at the neck with a large round metal buckle. He stared down at them with dark, unblinking eyes and a stern expression on his bearded face. In one hand he held a sword, still sheathed in its scabbard.

"You have passed the first test," he said, still without blinking. "Now for the second."

"We have to fight you?" Tia exclaimed with rising panic in her voice.

He raised an eyebrow, still looking severe. "Not unless you really want to." He held out the scabbard with the handle of the sword pointing towards them. "Just draw the sword."

"Is that the sword of Rhydderch Hael?" Tia asked.

The man nodded. "It is a test of worthiness," he said. "If you had come bearing arms, I would have presented you with the whetstone of Tudwal Tudglyd: the test of bravery." He gestured towards a large stone sitting in a hollow in the chamber wall to their left. "You would have sharpened your blade on it, and we would have done battle.

"If you had come claiming to be of noble birth, I would have presented you with the coat of Padarn Red-Coat: the test of nobility." He glanced over at a large tunic hanging on the wall to their right, which seemed to comprise more metal links than fabric. "You would have put it on and if you'd passed the test it would have shrunk to fit you. If you hadn't it would have gone on shrinking until you couldn't breathe." His voice was emotionless, as if the potential death of another person gave him no pleasure, yet caused him no alarm.

Tia gasped quietly in response to his words, while Pasco whimpered.

"But you didn't," the man continued, "and so your test is this." He extended the sheathed sword further towards them. "Draw the sword."

Tia looked at Pasco, who took a deep breath to steady his nerves before speaking.

"You do it, Tia. This is your quest, but I'll be with you whatever happens."

Tia's mind raced with thoughts of what might happen if she failed the test. Yet how could she turn away now? Her heart swelled at her friend's words. This was *her* quest.

She placed a hand on the pommel of the sword handle. It was warm to the touch. She took hold of it first in one hand, then two. The sword wasn't huge, but neither were Tia's hands. For a moment she thought about drawing it out slowly, but then she decided against it.

She took a deep breath and, in one swift movement, wrenched the blade free of its scabbard.

And yet the sword seemed to have no blade at all.

From the hilt to the tip was a silently rippling ruby-red flame. There was no hint of yellow or orange, just a pure red, like blood pumping through a completely transparent vein. Tia held it as close to her face as she dared, but was still unable to tell whether there was metal beneath the flame or not.

The man sighed.

Tia looked up at him. His eyes were shut, and his stern face had melted into an expression of blissful relief.

"Praise be," he whispered. Then he opened his eyes and turned to look over his shoulder. "Our watch is finished, brother."

Still holding the burning sword, Tia looked past the figure in front of her, and for the first time noticed there was another person in the chamber. He was, if anything, even larger than the first man and was dressed in a similar fashion, but without the bloodstains. He looked very like him, though not as severe. He smiled softly at the three of them.

The first brother held out the scabbard and nodded at Tia. She slid the flaming blade back inside it. When the last of the blood-red fire had disappeared, the chamber seemed to be plunged into darkness for a split second until the paler light of the blue torches reasserted itself.

Clutching the sheathed sword in his left hand, he strode across to the second man. The two shook hands by grasping one another's right forearms with their own and wrapping their other arms around each other's shoulders in a heartfelt embrace.

"I shall see you on the other side," said the first man. He turned to Tia and said, with tears in his eyes: "Thank you, child."

Then he strode over to a long, bed-like hollow cut in the side of the cavern and, with one final joyful look at his brother, climbed inside, laid the sword beside him, curled up and remained completely still.

Chapter Thirty

The Chamber of the Thirteen Treasures

Tia and Pasco gazed at the second man, unsure as to what they were expected to do next.

He smiled at them reassuringly. "My name is Sanddef, and that's my brother Bryd. We've been waiting for you for a very long time. Myrddin warned us it would be a long wait, but I don't think we realised just how long he meant." He paused to laugh softly to himself. "But you're finally here. You've already done so well… and yet there is so much more to do."

"The third test, you mean," said Tia.

"Yes," he said hesitantly, "but much more than that."

"Who are you?" Pasco asked.

"Yes, perhaps we should start there." He paused for a moment, then said brightly: "Come. Are you hungry or thirsty? Just take a sip from the drinking horn or lift the lid of that pot and you'll find whatever you desire inside. Carve it up with the knife or leave it to multiply in the hamper and you'll be able to eat all night. In fact, you could keep going for centuries. We have!"

Tia suddenly realised she hadn't eaten anything since breakfast, and even then she had only consumed a tiny amount. As well as being driven by hunger, she was curious to try out some of these treasures.

Pasco had already moved to the side of the table.

"Does the food from here keep you alive for hundreds of years, then?" Pasco asked, reaching for the pot and lifting the lid. "Wow," he whispered, pulling out a warm slice of pepperoni pizza.

"Not exactly." Sanddef was staring at Pasco, clearly never having seen pizza before.

Pasco set the slice down on the table and cut it in half with the knife. He handed one half to Tia, but somewhere between the table and her hand it grew to the size of a full slice without either seeing it happen. They glanced down at Pasco's half on the table and saw that it, too, was a full slice.

Tia took a bite and realised she would never be able to go back to takeaway pizza again. It was the most wonderful thing she had ever tasted. She looked up at Pasco, about to comment on his excellent choice of food, but he was busy chewing a mouthful with his eyes shut and a dreamy look on his face.

"It's the cauldron that has truly given us such long life," Sanddef continued, still staring at the pizza with a baffled look on his face.

"I thought the cauldron just showed whether you were brave by boiling or refusing to boil your meat," Tia said between mouthfuls.

"That's what it became famous for under its last owner, but when Dyrnwch the Giant first took possession of it, it had another power. With a little extra magic it can also sustain life, and that's what it was first famous for. It is a very ancient object. All these treasures stretch back much further than the time at which they were gathered together. As do my brother and I."

Pasco and Tia continued eating but turned their attention to the evidently ancient man standing before them to hear his story.

"In our day, the people of this land largely kept to their own tribes. Most of the interaction they had with other tribes was in combat. Then we were all threatened by invaders from another land, and we managed to convince all the tribes to unite in defence of our land. It was unheard of, but we, the sons of Angell, managed it. Together we drove our enemies away and a peace reigned across all the lands of the united tribes such that none had ever dreamed possible.

But war eventually came again, and this time we did not survive. My brother and I had been dead for many centuries when Myrddin came to wake us. He asked if he could use our tomb and if we would be prepared to guard something for him."

Tia was reminded of the history lesson her parents had given her in the kitchen a few weeks earlier. These brothers may have lived centuries before Arthur, but it seemed bizarre how closely their story reflected his. She wondered whether that was why Merlin had chosen them as guardians of the treasures.

"Myrddin came and went a few times during those early days," Sanddef continued. "He deposited various objects with us and took a few away with him. He told us that someday someone would come – a person we would not be expecting – and that if they passed the tests they would take the treasure away."

"We haven't passed all the tests yet, though, have we?" Tia said. She had finished her pizza and felt her appetite being chased away by the returning feeling of apprehension. "We still have the third test to face."

Pasco had also finished eating and didn't reach for any more.

"The third test is straightforward enough, and you will face it as you leave," the guardian said. "It's a simple test of honesty and integrity. All of this," he glanced around, pointing at all the treasures in the chamber, "has really all been for one treasure. The other twelve are just here to protect the one, and it is only this one that you are permitted to take away."

Tia could feel goosebumps rising on her arms.

"If you try to take any other treasure," Sanddef continued, "the spells that hold these earthen walls in place – indeed, the spells that hold back the very passing of time in this chamber – will be broken and the centuries that should have passed down here will suddenly catch up with us. That would make no difference to my brother or myself; our tasks are almost done. But yours are not."

Tia pondered his words for a moment. "Twelve of the treasures are only here to protect the thirteenth," she whispered.

"Well," said Pasco, "the gwyddbwyll was here for the first test."

"And the sword, the whetstone and the coat were here for the second test. The first guardian told us that," continued Tia.

"It looks like the knife, the hamper, the horn, the pot and the dish are all here to feed the brothers," said Pasco, "and the cauldron is here to keep them alive. That leaves the halter, the chariot and –"

Tia knew which one he was referring to and finished Pasco's sentence for him: "The Mantle of Arthur."

It was the only treasure whose owner she'd had no trouble remembering. The sword of Rhydderch Hael had always intrigued her – and did so even more now that it had considered her worthy enough to burst into flame – but it was this thirteenth treasure that had most captivated her imagination and had always seemed more sacred than the rest.

"The Mantle of Arthur," Sanddef echoed softly, pulling a bundle of black material out from under his cloak. "We thought we would lose our minds down here," he continued in a lighter tone, "until Myrddin brought us the halter." He motioned over to where a horse's bridle hung on the wall. "But with that we were able to summon a magical steed capable of carrying one of us out of here, through these very walls, so that we could taste fresh air every now and then. We had to return before dusk each time before the horse vanished into the night."

Still holding the bundle reverently in his hands, Sanddef strode over to the chariot, which stood beside the table. "The chariot, however, is for a one-way journey. It's for the two of you when you're ready to leave. Just step inside, and in the blink of an eye you will be transported straight up, through all the physical and magical barriers, and without any harm, into the open air."

Tia and Pasco walked over to join him.

"What will happen to you and Bryd afterwards?" Tia asked.

"We will rest," he said in a soft voice, beaming at her.

"You mean you'll die," she said hesitantly.

"We have already died," he said simply.

Tia waited for a moment, wondering whether the guardian would give any further explanation, but he said nothing more. He was still holding the folded black cloak out before him. Tia laid a hand on top of it, but before she could pick it up Sanddef placed a strong, rough hand on top of hers.

"Myrddin charged me with one further task," he said. "To give you a message."

Sanddef gazed at her with round, dark eyes. It would have been impossible to look away, even if Tia had wanted to.

"With your coming," he continued, "the time is now at hand for the Hallows of Arthur to be gathered – for unity not division; for love not war; for creation not destruction; for grace not law. This is your task: to gather the Hallows of Arthur."

"That's it?" asked Tia, looking bewildered. "What on earth does that mean?"

"I'm sorry, child. I was only given the message, not the meaning. But Myrddin did say one more thing that will hopefully prove more helpful…"

But before he could say what the other thing was, two men burst out of the tunnel and into the chamber. They were tall and square with masses of curly hair and thick arms. They looked vaguely familiar to Tia, but she didn't have long enough to place them. Immediately after entering the chamber, they stepped aside and a third figure wearing an immaculate suit stepped out of the tunnel between them. A person she remembered with haunting clarity.

"Hello again, Tia," said Mr Silverman in his slithery, serpentine voice.

Chapter Thirty-One

The Third Test

A triumphant smile spread across Mr Silverman's face as his eyes fell on each of the treasures in turn. "Remarkable," he whispered to himself.

His two henchmen were staring at the guardian, who was standing beside the chariot with Tia and Pasco.

"Are you friends or foes?" Sanddef asked the newcomers in a hard voice he hadn't used with Tia and Pasco.

"Foes," Tia answered for them.

"Come now, Tia," Mr Silverman drawled, still smiling. "You never even gave me a chance to be friendly at our last meeting. We might have got along splendidly if you hadn't run off like that." He rubbed the hand where Tia had bitten him, looking down at it thoughtfully.

Tia wondered whether she had left a scar. She was reminded not only of how menacing Mr Silverman had seemed, but of how brave she had been.

He seemed to remember too, and decided to take necessary precautions. "Tie them up," he said, no longer smiling.

The two henchmen advanced, one walking around the table and a slightly shorter man coming directly toward them, both still fixing their gaze on Sanddef. They clearly intended to subdue him first before turning their attention to Tia and Pasco.

If only the first brother would wake up, thought Tia, though she suspected that he wasn't merely sleeping.

Sanddef hadn't moved a muscle. He simply stared straight ahead, trying to hold both henchmen at the edge of his vision. The taller man, who had been moving around the table, was standing directly in front of Tia but still hadn't so much as glanced at her. She summoned all the strength she had and swung a foot into his shin as hard and swiftly as she could.

Within a split-second, Sanddef had thrown an elbow into the face of the second henchman and launched himself on top of him. The pair began grappling on the floor while the man Tia had kicked lunged towards her. She darted to one side, but as he fell to the floor the man managed to grab hold of her ankle.

"Stop!"

Tia looked up to see Mr Silverman twisting Pasco's arm up behind his back with one hand, the other holding the knife of Llawfrodedd the Horseman against his throat. Pasco was as white as a ghost.

"Now, let's try that again," Mr Silverman said smoothly.

The two henchmen tied Sanddef's hands behind his back before doing the same to Tia. Once they were securely bound, Mr Silverman released Pasco from his grasp and his hands were also tied. The three captives were then forced to the ground and made to sit against the back wall.

They weren't sitting far from the chariot, and it looked to Tia as though she and Pasco might be able to throw themselves on to it, despite their bonds. But she was determined not to leave without Arthur's cloak, which lay on the ground a little to the other side of them, in the opposite direction from the chariot. She figured it would be too difficult to grab it and make it back to the chariot before being noticed.

"Right," Mr Silverman said, addressing his cronies, "remember what I said. We need to handle all these artefacts very carefully. Her Ladyship will not be pleased if anything gets damaged. Everything must be carefully wrapped and packed so we can carry it out of here safely. Iago, fetch the boxes. Iolo, bring the cauldron over."

The shorter man, Iago, disappeared into the tunnel and came back carrying two crates. He opened one, which appeared to be full of straw, then went over to the table and picked up the drinking horn.

"Who's *Her Ladyship*?" Tia asked. She knew Mr Silverman was unlikely to tell her, but she was trying to buy some time while one of them came up with a plan. She suspected the spell would be broken the moment any treasure was taken into the tunnel, and she wanted to get away before that happened.

"I don't think we'll need to carry anything inside this after all," Mr Silverman continued, ignoring Tia and inspecting the cauldron Iolo had brought over. "It's a little smaller than I was expecting." He handed the knife of Llawfrodedd the Horseman to Iago, who packed it into the crate along with the horn.

"You won't be able to take any of those with you."

Tia wasn't sure whether Sanddef was also playing for time, or whether he was just issuing them with the third test as part of his duty, but he succeeded in halting the three men.

"What do you mean?" demanded Mr Silverman, his eyes narrowing.

"It's the test of honesty and integrity," Sanddef continued coolly. "Only one treasure may be removed from this chamber. If you try to take any of the others the enchantments holding the roof above our heads will break and we will all be buried alive."

Iago and Iolo looked nervously at Mr Silverman, who continued to stare at the guardian. It was then that Tia noticed Sanddef had pulled a tiny flint blade out from somewhere and had almost cut through the rope used to tie his wrists together behind his back.

"I don't believe you," Mr Silverman said sharply after a long pause.

"Then your fate is sealed," the guardian said simply.

Mr Silverman turned towards his henchmen. "Put the cauldron in and seal up that crate…"

Sanddef had cut through the last thread of rope.

"Iago, you take it up while Iolo and I put the rest of the things in the other crate."

The guardian, his eyes still fixed on Mr Silverman, who had noticed nothing, was slowly moving into a crouched position.

"I have no idea how we're going to get the chariot out," continued Mr Silverman, "but if we can't do it tonight, we'll just leave it here. I'm not coming back."

Sanddef edged a hand out towards the cloak as Iago lifted the sealed crate and headed for the chamber's entrance. He hesitated at the mouth of the passageway for a moment, then stepped into the tunnel.

The ground instantly began to shake. Dust fell from the ceiling, then great lumps of earth. There was a rumbling sound that grew steadily louder. Mr Silverman, Iolo and Iago started shouting, but their voices were drowned out as the rumbles and roars grew ever louder.

Tia saw the table turn to dust and the treasures that had been sitting on it crash to the floor. She could no longer see Mr Silverman through the thick clouds of dry earth dropping all around them.

In the chaos, Sanddef managed to grab the cloak and leap back towards Tia and Pasco.

"Stone! Oak! Circle!" he yelled in Tia's ear to make himself heard above the deafening sound of the collapsing chamber. He stuffed the bundled cloak under Pasco's jumper, and in a single motion tucked a child under each of his huge arms, spun around and threw himself towards the chariot.

Tia had expected to hit the hard wood of the chariot's bottom, but instead she felt cold, soft soil beneath her. The horrific noise of the cave-in had vanished in an instant, and there was nothing but the sound of her own panting. For a dreadful moment Tia thought that she had been buried alive, but then she realised she was surrounded by cool air rather than earth, and that it was only pitch black because her eyes were screwed tightly shut.

She opened them.

It was much darker than it had been when they were last above ground, but there was still a lingering dim light behind the grey clouds overhead. Tia looked about her. She was in a field and Pasco was there next to her. To her left she could see the village and its church sitting there peacefully, blissfully unaware of what had just happened beneath the ground.

They had escaped.

"Pasco! We're alive!"

Pasco opened and closed his mouth but seemed unable to speak.

Chapter Thirty-Two

Back to the Church

Once Pasco had recovered a little, they sat back to back and untied each other's hands. This took some time, as they had been tightly bound.

As they sat there, Tia wondered what had become of the men in the chamber below them. Sanddef seemed content that his time was coming to an end anyway, but what of Mr Silverman and his henchmen?

She shuddered and tried to think of something else.

How long had she and Pasco been underground? Was it minutes or hours? Night still hadn't quite fallen, so it couldn't have been any longer than an hour or two... unless it had been several days. Tia couldn't tell either way.

Once they were both free, the pair stood up and Pasco pulled the bundled cloak out from under his jumper. He paused before handing it to Tia.

"The Mantle of Arthur," she said in a hushed voice.

"You remember what the legend says it can do, right?" said Pasco excitedly.

Tia nodded, wondering what invisibility would feel like.

She opened it out. It was a large, hooded black cloak that appeared quite plain, with just a metal hook and loop to tie it around the neck. She swept it over her shoulders and fastened it under her chin, the hem dragging along the floor.

Nothing even remotely magical happened. Pasco could definitely still see her.

"Do you think the spell broke when Mr Silverman and his men tried taking the other treasures?" Pasco suggested.

"I don't know," said Tia, feeling rather disappointed. She had hoped the cloak would be proof of everything that had happened. She wasn't even sure her family would believe them, let alone anyone else, if all they had to show for it was a plain black cloak that looked little more than a few years old.

"Let's get back to the church," she said, taking off the cloak and packing it into her backpack. "Nana's probably wondering where we've got to."

"Hold on," said Pasco, bending down to gather up

the ropes that had tied their hands behind their backs. He dug a shallow hole in the loose soil with his hand and half buried the ropes with a few ends sticking out into the air, like the leafless stems of a strange vegetable, as a way of marking the spot.

"He said the chariot would transport us straight up," Pasco explained, standing up and brushing the dirt from his hands, "which means the treasure chamber is directly below us. Even if it's caved in and time has caught up with it, there'll still be a lot of stuff down there to excavate."

Tia beamed at him. "Brilliant, Pasco!"

It took them some time to get back to the village, as they had to trudge across two muddy fields before they reached a path. They saw the little Trevelyan car parked exactly where it had been outside the church.

At first there appeared to be no sign of Nana Ollie and Meghan.

The pair walked into the church and both instinctively looked over at the font, but it had returned to its original position. Tia glanced at Pasco, then crouched down and placed her hand on the Solomon's knot carving. This time it was cold. Nothing happened.

"The spells have been broken," said Pasco.

"I wonder if Mr Silverman and his thugs made it out," said Tia.

"Did you recognise the other two?" Pasco asked.

"No, just their leader."

"I think I did."

"What?" Tia spun around and stared at him.

"I think they were staying at the youth hostel," Pasco said, frowning. "They must have been following us since this morning."

"But how did they know we were up here in Yorkshire at all?"

"That's what I was thinking," he said, still frowning. "The police thought the burglar at your house might have been someone living in Stormhaven, right? What if she's been spying on you and saw us leaving yesterday?"

"Maybe she followed us up here and told the others," Tia said, thinking aloud.

"Or she knew we were heading here some other way," said Pasco in an ominous tone.

Tia wondered if he had already come to the same conclusion she had just arrived at. For the last week, Meghan had been telling everyone who would listen that they were travelling to Kirkburn on a treasure hunt. Everyone at Stormhaven Castle would have known where to find them if they had wanted to.

Tia's thoughts were interrupted by a banging noise coming from the top of the narrow staircase Meghan had wanted to climb when they first entered the church. She and Pasco carefully climbed the steps and came to a large wooden door with a chair jammed under the handle so it couldn't be opened from the inside. With some effort, Tia and Pasco heaved the chair away and opened the door.

"Oh, thank goodness!" cried Nana Ollie as she rushed out of the tiny room and threw her arms around Tia. "What on earth happened?"

"We came into the church to look for you," Meghan said, exploding out of the room in a rush of words, "but we couldn't see you downstairs, so I thought you'd come up here, but when we came up the door slammed shut behind us and we couldn't get it open, and we were stuck in there for ages."

"Someone shut you in," Tia said darkly, motioning towards the chair. "That was wedged against the door."

Nana Ollie and Meghan stared at the chair in silence for a moment. Apparently, they'd had no suspicion of this, and had assumed the old door was simply stuck.

"What happened to you two?" the old lady asked warily, looking at their filthy clothes and faces.

Tia considered whether to tell them the whole incredible story. She didn't feel she could trust Meghan not to tell the world, and she knew that very few people would believe it. There was also the fact that there seemed to be someone at Stormhaven who wished her ill and could be anywhere right now.

"Can we go back to the hostel?" she asked.

Nana Ollie gave a concerned frown.

"We're okay, honestly," Tia added reassuringly. "I'd

just like to get somewhere warm and cosy before we tell you all about it."

Her grandmother looked unsure but agreed. Meghan looked incredulous, clearly desperate to know what had happened, but she silently relented and the four of them descended the stone steps.

"Did you notice anything strange when you came back into the church, Nana?" Tia asked quietly as they passed the font.

"To tell you the truth, I didn't get the chance to notice anything," she answered in a whisper. "Your sister came in first and was already disappearing up the steps when I came through the door, so I just went after her as quickly as I could."

Tia wondered whether the tunnel under the font had still been open when her grandmother re-entered the church. She supposed it had to have been and they just hadn't noticed it, otherwise Mr Silverman wouldn't have been able to shut them in the room before coming after Tia and Pasco. Unless someone else had imprisoned them, she mused. One thing was certain: if the tunnel entrance had already sealed itself by the time Nana Ollie and Meghan had returned to the church, Mr Silverman and his cronies could not have escaped. Tia shuddered at the thought once more.

Chapter Thirty-Three

Questions, Answers and More Questions

Exhausted, Tia and Pasco fell asleep during the drive and woke with a start when the car stopped outside the hostel. Tia suddenly thought of the two henchmen Pasco had recognised. Perhaps they'd escaped and were waiting for them there. If they hadn't, perhaps it would be possible to go through whatever they'd left behind in their room to find some clues as to who they were.

Tia leaned forward, frantically grabbing at everyone to stop them getting out of the car. Then she and Pasco briefly explained about the two men who had been staying at the hostel.

Nana Ollie went to speak to the hostel warden and returned within a couple of minutes. "They packed up and left soon after we did this morning," she reported back. "They only stayed the one night. The warden thought they were very shifty, though. Barely spoke, apparently, even to each other."

Tia sighed. It was a relief not to have to worry about them either way. It was dark now and getting colder all the time. They dragged themselves inside, and Tia and Pasco washed and changed while Nana Ollie ordered Chinese takeaway from a menu pinned to a board in the communal lounge area. They were the only people staying at the hostel, so they had the place to themselves that evening as Tia and Pasco retold their adventures between mouthfuls of chicken chow mein.

Tia explained how they thought Mr Silverman had found them, hoping to impress upon Meghan that it might be better not to go around telling anyone and everyone the details of their expedition. Tia noticed that her sister looked rather downcast at this point, so she hoped she had made her point.

Then she continued with the events that had followed their re-entering the church. If Nana Ollie doubted the authenticity of her story, she didn't voice it. Instead, she listened quietly, looking intently at her granddaughter all the while. Meghan was equally silent but seemed unable to meet Tia's eye.

Tia decided not to retell every part of the story. She didn't mention Sanddef's message from Merlin, or Myrddin as he had called him. Neither did she reveal what he had said about the Mantle of Arthur being the most important treasure, intentionally giving the impression that they had escaped empty-handed. She wanted to make out that the whole adventure had now come to a tidy end; that the Thirteen Treasures marked the end of the trail and the bad guys had not escaped.

"I understand why you wanted to pretend it's all finished now," said Pasco as they shuffled off to bed, leaving Meghan and Nana Ollie to tidy up the lounge. "It'll stop them worrying and I guess it means Meghan can't let anything else slip." He flopped onto his bed as soon as they entered the bedroom. "It would be nice to think it's all over," he said in a muffled voice as he lay with his cheek on his pillow, "but it's not, is it?"

"No," Tia answered, but Pasco was already asleep.

Tia felt exhausted, but her mind was crackling with thoughts. The light was still on in the room, so she took out her journal and started writing down all the things the second brother had said, in the hope that it would still her mind and enable her to get some sleep.

She was also very conscious of the fact that she didn't understand the cryptic message Merlin had left with Sanddef. Although the details were still fresh in her mind, she knew she would soon forget them if she continued to omit them when recounting her story.

Turning to the next empty page, she wrote:

> *The guardian's message from Merlin/Myrddin:*
> *With your coming, the time is now at hand*
> *for the Hallows of Arthur to be gathered*
> *for unity not division; for love not war;*
> *for creation not destruction; for grace not law.*
> *This is your task: to gather the Hallows of Arthur.*

She wasn't sure why she had written it out like a poem, but this somehow made her feel a bit better about not fully understanding it. She had always found poetry a little tricky to unpick, yet she loved the rhythm of verse. It felt as though these words needed to be written as a poem.

Then she wrote down the three words the guardian had shouted just before throwing them to safety:

> *Stone. Oak. Circle.*

She sighed. Yet again she was left with more questions than answers, but at least she was feeling drowsy now. She put the journal back in her bag, climbed into bed without bothering to turn off the light, and fell asleep almost before her eyelids closed.

"Do you believe me?" Tia asked her parents, who were sitting either side of her on the living room sofa.

They had barely moved while she was giving them the same explanation of events she had given Nana Ollie and Meghan twenty-four hours earlier. They looked at one another before responding.

"It just all sounds so remarkable, Tia," her mother began hesitantly.

"I know," Tia said earnestly. "But it's all true, I promise!"

Mr and Mrs Trevelyan glanced at each other again, clearly unsure what to make of it all.

"I just wish I knew why all this has happened." Tia could feel tears coming as she continued and tried to blink them back. "Why me?"

"Tia," her father said softly, taking her hands in his. "We trust you. Just give us a little time to process all this."

Tia had no idea how long Mr and Mrs Trevelyan and Nana Ollie spent talking about her story that night once she and Meghan had gone up to bed, her sister still avoiding eye contact with her. The following day, however, Tia received proof of her parents' trust in her, even if they were still finding it hard to believe all the incredible details.

When he returned home after work, Mr Trevelyan informed her that he had been to see Dougal Dinsmore, and that they were organising a team of archaeologists from Stormhaven to excavate the field Pasco had marked up in Yorkshire.

"I left out as many details of your story as I could," he reassured her. "I said just enough to convince him that it would be worth the trip. We leave next week."

Chapter Thirty-Four

The Key

A few weeks later, at the start of the Christmas holidays, Tia found herself standing in front of a glass cabinet at the British Museum in London. The cabinet displayed a blackened but beautiful sword. It was almost unrecognisable from the flaming blade she had drawn from its scabbard. But as she moved around, looking at it from different angles, the reflection of her fiery red hair in the glass would dance along the length of the sword every so often, almost making it look as though it were ablaze once more.

Beside the sword lay three spearheads. The information beside the display case explained that the warrior the sword had been buried alongside had been stabbed with three spears. Tia thought of the three bloodstained holes on Bryd's tunic, and an icy feeling came over her.

The only other exhibit on display that had been recovered from the excavation was a pair of pins that had been part of the chariot she and Pasco had used to escape from the collapsing chamber. Many more items had been dug up by the team of archaeologists from Stormhaven, but they were safely stowed somewhere within the museum's vaults.

It seemed as though fragments of almost all the other treasures had been found: many more fragments of the chariot, pieces of pottery from the pot and dish, metallic decorations from the lid of the hamper, loops from the bridle, a metal link from the coat and the entire whetstone. The sword seemed to be the most exciting piece to the experts, however, just as it was to Tia.

The gwyddbwyll pieces were safe in Tia's possession, but few people knew of them, and Pasco was the only other person who knew about the cloak. It seemed the only objects there was no trace of were the ones that had been packed into the crate by Mr Silverman and his henchmen: the cauldron, the horn and the knife. The men must have made it out of the chamber somehow, because only two skeletons were discovered there. With a shiver, Tia wondered how far along the tunnel they had managed to get.

Altogether, the finds had proved extremely valuable

and had generated some much-needed income for Stormhaven. Tia hoped this had significantly damaged Llacheu Thunderford's schemes to turn the castle into a hotel. This was the most satisfying outcome of the adventure for Tia, as she had been rather disappointed that the treasure trove hadn't been given a more prominent position at the British Museum.

Her father, who had been bouncing with excitement for days after returning from the dig, tried to reassure her of how wonderful the find was. "This is probably the finest Iron Age sword in Europe," he had told her.

Yet somehow that didn't come close to capturing the magic of the story behind it.

Tia had been lingering in this room for quite some time. She began to wonder how many other items on display had incredible stories behind them and thought that she perhaps shouldn't be so dismissive of other treasures in the building.

She moved away from her sword and gazed for a while at a beautifully decorated bronze helmet with two enormous straight horns sprouting from it. The caption declared that it was the only horned helmet from this point in history to have been discovered anywhere in the world. She longed for another two-thousand-year-old man to sidle up to her and tell her the tale of this unique piece of history, just as the two brothers had been able to tell her about the Thirteen Treasures.

Two small boys came running up to the Kirkburn Sword and pressed their faces against the glass.

"Cor, look at that!" said the first, almost shouting with excitement.

"Whoa," said the second in an awed voice. "I bet that sword belonged to a warrior king who fought giants and dragons!"

Tia smiled to herself and crept up behind them. "This is White-Hilt, the legendary sword of Rhydderch Hael," she said in what she hoped was a mystical voice. "If the magical sword was drawn out of its scabbard by an unworthy person it would just produce a dull metal blade; but if it was drawn by someone worthy, it would burst into flames the colour of blood and burn so fiercely you couldn't see the blade at all. Rhydderch would offer the sword to anyone, but almost all were too afraid to draw it in case it deemed them unworthy."

As Tia spoke, the boys' heads slowly turned and their mouths opened.

"Wow!" they whispered in unison before running off, giggling and chattering excitedly to each other. Feeling satisfied with their response, Tia left the room in search of her parents and sister, who were downstairs in the museum's Great Court.

The three of them had been in quite different moods since the girls' adventures in Kirkburn. Mr Trevelyan had been in a permanent state of excitement over the finds, while Mrs Trevelyan just felt deeply relieved that, following the apparent demise of Mr Silverman, the dangerous aspect of the mystery surrounding Geoffrey Hemyke appeared to be over.

Tia wondered whether the burglar was still in Stormhaven, but felt fairly sure he or she had just been working for Mr Silverman. Besides, she wasn't about to mention anything that might make Mrs Trevelyan worry again. Her mother had suggested that they all join Mr Trevelyan in Aberystwyth in the New Year to find out what they could about Tia's connection to Hemyke's research.

Meghan had been unnaturally quiet for a few weeks. Since returning from their treasure hunt, she had only really talked to people about finding the field and the planned excavation, and even then she didn't talk with her customary zeal.

Tia felt a pang of guilt every time she looked at her sister. She knew Meghan deeply regretted how unrestrained she had been in talking to anyone and everyone about their trip to Yorkshire before they went. Tia greatly missed her sister's energy and enthusiasm, and wished she hadn't made it quite so clear that Meghan was most likely to blame for their misadventure.

As Tia entered the brightness of the museum's Great Court she could see her father and sister moving off towards another exhibit, leaving her mother to wait for her. Tia was too far away to truly tell, but she felt sure that Meghan's shoulders were drooping again, and a cold surge of guilt washed over her.

"Ah, there you are, Tia," Mrs Trevelyan said, smiling serenely at her. "The other two have just gone off to look at the Africa exhibit. Shall we go after them?"

"I think I'd prefer to just wait here for them," she said wearily.

"Meghan will cheer up soon," her mother said, guessing why Tia looked so glum. "I don't think you'd have seen it before, but Meghan can be really hard on herself at times. Whenever she realises she's gone too far she beats herself up about how excitable she gets. She just needs us to appreciate her for who she is, despite all the chaos she sometimes brings with her."

"I *do* appreciate her!" Tia groaned. "I wish she was back to her old self *so* much!"

"Just give her time," Mrs Trevelyan said softly, "and make it clear that you still love her. She'll soon be back to normal."

They sat down on a step and Mrs Trevelyan took out a notepad and pencil. "Meghan worked something out a couple of days ago," she said after some hesitation. "We've been trying to get her to tell you about it herself, but… well, it's probably time that I showed you."

She wrote TIA HEMYKE on a blank page and then rearranged the letters, crossing each one out as she rewrote it below:

~~TIA HEMYKE~~
I AM THE KEY

"*Meghan* worked this out?" she eventually said, immediately hating herself for sounding as though she doubted her sister's ability to decipher something like this. "I mean –"

"Yes," said her mother warmly but hurriedly, so as to spare Tia the awkwardness she felt. "Meghan had been puzzling over how you managed to open the tunnel in the church, and that's when she discovered this. Your father and I think you might be the 'key' Professor Hemyke had been talking about. Now, we can't really tell whether he discovered your ability before he died, or whether someone else left you in Ms Davidson's care, but we may get some answers in Aberystwyth in a couple of weeks' time."

Tia let out a sigh. She couldn't even work out how she felt. This discovery seemed to place a special importance on her, yet it made her feel incredibly small and powerless at the same time. She sighed and leaned against her mother for comfort.

"I don't understand it either, Tia," Mrs Trevelyan said as she held her daughter close. "But there's clearly some sort of magic at work that I didn't believe existed until a few weeks ago. Just remember you're not alone. We're still going to do all we can to help you find whatever answers you choose to look for."

After some time resting against her mother, Tia resolved to talk to Meghan on her own when she next had the chance, and to confide in her the aspects of the story that only she and Pasco knew. She would show her the journal, and tell her about the cloak and everything Sanddef had said. She could think of no better way of getting the old Meghan, whom she so longed for, back.

With this plan in mind Tia was able to grin broadly at her sister when she returned to the Great Court with their father. She thought she saw Meghan's shoulders lift a little in response, and for a moment Meghan's eyes seemed to find some of their old sparkle again.

The Trevelyans gathered up their things and then the family of four – brought together by something more than birth and blood – left the museum together and stepped out into the crisp December afternoon.

The Real-Life Treasures Mentioned in This Book

At the time of writing, the Kirkburn Sword is on display in the British Museum as described, with the other artefacts mentioned held in storage, but exhibits are subject to change over time.

The Capricorn figurine is on display at the Museum of Somerset in Taunton, and a 3D model of it was created by the University of Exeter for the 2020 Festival of Archaeology Digital Week in partnership with South West Heritage.

The Jamaica Inn museum on Bodmin Moor and Wilberforce House in Hull are both wonderful small museums and well worth a visit.

The font marking the entrance to the chamber of the Thirteen Treasures of Britain is in position at St Mary's parish church in Kirkburn, complete with the Solomon's knot carving. It can be found using the longitude and latitude co-ordinates written on the inside of Tia's treasure pouch.

Activities

There are oodles of potential cross-curricular links in the Tales of Truth and Treasure series that will provide readers with a more immersive experience and enrich children's learning. Here are a few ideas for schoolteachers, home educators and curious readers that tie in with events in *The Lost Child's Quest*. The activity doesn't need to be completed at the end of the corresponding chapter, but it won't make much sense to do it beforehand.

I believe that children learn best when their senses are engaged, and when their bodies and brains are stimulated. I hope these ideas will help my readers achieve that, and will inspire and excite them to dream, create, learn and grow.

Chapter One

Read the description of Tia at the start of chapter one. She has "large round eyes the colour of a stormy sea". We're going to have a go at painting one of Tia's eyes.

Firstly, use a mirror to look carefully at the shape and detail of your own eyes. Find a pencil and some watercolour paper to sketch a larger version of your eye. Start by drawing a round circle for the iris (you could draw around a cup if that's easier – drawing circles freehand is surprisingly difficult!). Then add a smaller circle inside it for the black pupil (you could draw round an egg cup for this). You will then need a curved line above and below the iris to create the full shape of the eye. Add eyelashes, an eyelid, a tear duct and maybe an eyebrow.

When you're ready to start painting, think carefully about the colours you can use or mix to create the colour of a 'stormy sea', like Tia's eyes. Remember that your idea of what that means may not be the same as someone else's.

Chapter Two

Have you ever played Top Trumps? What ratings would you give Mr Silverman for speed, strength and aggression? What else would you give him ratings for calmness, trickery or intelligence, perhaps?

Try to find specific pieces of descriptive language to support the ratings you have given. You could even draw out a Top Trumps card for Mr Silverman complete with a sketch of what you think he looks like.

If you were to do the same for Tia, what ratings would you give her?

Chapter Three

Safety is a key theme in this chapter. What does safety look like to Tia? What does it look like to you?

Without family, friends or community, people feel very unsafe. It's a human right to feel safe whatever your gender, language, religion, ethnicity or ability level. Feeling safe means you don't need to worry about neglect or abuse. It means you are confident that your basic needs, such as food and drink, healthcare, education, rest and play, will be met. Can you draw or build what an ideal safe environment looks like to you? It doesn't have to be a literal representation of a place. It could be an artistic arrangement of things that make you feel safe, or that suggest safety to you.

Even if we have lots of people and things around us that help us feel safe, there may be other things that make us worry or feel unsafe, and that's completely natural. If you have any worries or concerns for your safety, please share them with an adult you trust and know in person.

Chapter Four

According to Tia, Stormhaven Castle is "a bit like a motte-and-bailey castle". Have a look at a few images of motte-and-bailey castles to get an idea of what was special about this design. Then have another read of Tia's first impressions and look at the map of Stormhaven Castle at the front of the book. Which part of Stormhaven is Tia thinking of as the motte and which part is the bailey?

Can you design your own motte-and-bailey castle? The lower courtyard needs a gateway and a few buildings. These would have originally been stables and houses for soldiers and others who worked at the castle, but in our story they are the thatched buildings where the archaeologists and historians work. From the courtyard you need to make a wooden bridge leading to a 'motte' (which means 'hill') with a 'keep' on it, which is like a mini castle. Can you make your castle? You could make it out of Lego, cardboard or just about anything else you like; even cake (I like cake).

Chapter Five

Tia spends her first evening in Stormhaven listening to Grandpa Locryn and the Trevelyans telling her all about her uncles, aunts and cousins.

Write out the names of as many of your family members as you can on small pieces of coloured paper – aunts, uncles, cousins, too. Your coloured paper could be leaf-, fruit- or heart-shaped. Now try arranging these on a big sheet of paper as a family tree, ensuring the older generation appears higher than the younger.

Remember that the Trevelyan family was brought together by more than birth and blood. Your family tree may include people who are not related to you by birth because that is not the only thing that makes people family.

Chapter Six

Activity one: Tia experiences her first Sunday morning service at the local chapel in this chapter. Your local place of worship may or may not be like the chapel at Stormhaven. Why not visit a place of worship that is unfamiliar to you? What do you think of the art, architecture or furniture? Tia is struck by the stained-glass windows in Stormhaven Chapel. Stained-glass windows were often used to tell stories, show important beliefs and inspire people at a time when not everyone could read.

Can you design your own special window to inspire others or share your beliefs? You could create the classic arched window shape by cutting an outline from black card, then fill your background with brightly coloured tissue paper to create "swirling chunks of vibrant colour" like the windows in this story. You could even add a silhouetted image or symbol to this colourful backdrop.

Activity two: Grandpa Locryn tells the story of how Jesus recruited his disciples. See what you can find out about who the disciples were and what their roles in society were before they followed Jesus. Put yourself in their shoes and consider how his invitation would have made them feel, and how it changed their lives.

Chapter Seven

There is a lot of action in this chapter, and it could be a really fun scene to act out with a partner. Start by focusing on your favourite section and turn it into a playscript to follow. Remember that speech and action look a bit different in a playscript. You might need notes about body language and equipment to use as props.

Try acting it out, and have some fun experimenting and creating a mini scene with your partner. You could even film it to analyse your performance.

Chapter Eight

It's your turn to become an archaeologist, but first you need to make a dig box. You could make a small one in a shoe box or a larger one in a paddling pool. Fill it with sand or soil. What could you hide? Some old coins, pieces of broken pottery or fossils, for example. Invite a friend to see what they can find by digging carefully with small tools and brushes. Try not to touch the artefacts with your bare hands as you remove them, and brush or scrape away the sand or soil around it before you lift it out. If any moves when the object is removed, you're in danger of damaging your artefact! As each item is discovered, discuss together what it could be. What might it have been used for? How old is it and what could it tell you about the people of the time?

Museums will sometimes have schemes where they lend out a box of artefacts relating to a specific period in history. Don't bury these items in a dig box, though!

Chapter Nine

The number thirteen is important in this story. Eight of Tia's thirteen treasures have circles on them, while five (including the pendant) have crosses, giving us the simple sum 5 + 8 = 13. These three numbers – 5, 8 and 13 – form part of a famous sequence. Do you know the name of it, and can you describe how it works?

Can you write out all the pairs of numbers that add up to 13? Do you notice anything about these pairs? Are they odd or even? Do the same for pairs of numbers that total 12. What do you notice about these pairs?

Can you come up with a rule for which two sorts of number you need to add together to make an odd number and an even number? Can you explain *why* this is the case?

Chapter Ten

In this chapter we are introduced to two old Welsh names: Llacheu and Gwydre. What do you know about Wales? Can you identify where it is on a map? What do you know about their flag?

Welsh pronunciations are very different from English ones. Here are a few words and phrases for non-Welsh speakers to try, but I suggest finding some online videos (or, even better, a real live Welsh person!) for accurate pronunciation.

c – pronounced 'k', as in 'kick'.

ch – pronounced as in the Scottish word 'loch' or the name of the composer Bach.

eu, ei – pronounced as the 'ay' in pray.

g – always pronounced as a hard 'g', as in 'get'.

i – pronounced 'ee', as in 'queen'.

ll – roughly pronounced 'hl'. Place your tongue firmly at the top of the mouth behind your teeth, then blow.

oe – pronounced as the 'oy' in 'toy'.

w – pronounced 'oo', as in 'spoon'.

y – usually pronounced 'u', as in 'fun', but pronounced 'i', as in 'is' in the last syllable of a word. So the Welsh for 'mountain', *mynydd*, is pronounced 'mun-ith', but the plural is *mynyddoedd*, pronounced 'mun-uth-oith' because the 'y' is no longer in the last syllable!

Have a go at saying these Welsh words and phrases:
Cymru (kumm-ree) – Wales
Bore da (bore-ray-dah) – Good morning
Nos da (Nohs-dah) – Good night
[Name] *dw i* (doo-ee) – I am [Name]
Helô/Hylô (hell-oh/hill-oh) – Hello
Hwyl (Hoy-ul) – Bye
Diolch (dee-olch) – Thanks
Croeso (croy-so) – Welcome

Chapter Eleven

Try playing a game of Halo. You will need two sticks (hockey sticks would work well) and a quoit (ring) made from rubber or stiff rope. Divide into two teams, with one player from each team, the goalkeeper, standing at either end of the playing area holding a stick. This goalkeeper must remain on a specific spot, with an area around them at least as far as they can reach with their stick, into which no one else is allowed.

Each team has to pass the quoit around (you can't move when you have the quoit) and try to throw it onto the end of their team's stick. You can't snatch it out of an opposing player's hands; you can only block a pass. If there is any dispute over who has possession of the quoit, the referee throws it up for a player from each team to contest (this is also done from the centre spot to start the game or after a score).

Have fun!

Chapter Twelve

Pasco is a bit worried that they don't attend a 'real' school. Do you think it sounds like a proper school? What do you think the point of school is, and what are the important things children need to learn? What does a good school look like? Can you do school at home?

Come up with a list of answers you think people might give if they were asked, "What does a school need to be good?" Is it the facilities, good teachers, fun activities, nice lunches, strict rules, a good library, laptops, a playground or something else? Once you have some ideas, create a poll and ask your family, neighbours or friends what they think. Decide how many things they can vote for and how to display your results.

Chapter Thirteen

Activity one: Tia and Paso reveal parts of their life stories in this chapter and are involved in a school project where they depict some of this in the style of the Bayeux Tapestry.

Choose an event from your life that you could depict in this style. It could be a holiday, the birth of a sibling, a sad death or a great experience or achievement. Make some notes or sketches before you begin, checking you have the order right. Add a border before carefully drawing your event in three or four pictures. Add as much detail as you can to your pictures. Finally, choose which objects you would like to add to the border around your work to represent your home, town, village or family. You could even have a go at sewing a personal tapestry onto a piece of hessian, like the Bayeux Tapestry (you can sketch a rough design out on hessian with a pencil to give you lines to follow with a needle and thread).

Activity two: Try sketching an object that is unfamiliar to you, so you really need to look at it carefully to draw it. If it is a completely unknown object, think about the design and what it could be used for (use your imagination – it doesn't have to be the right answer). If you're doing this activity in a group, each of you could bring something from home that you think others might not know the purpose of and would be interesting to draw.

Chapter Fourteen

Here are a few more ways in which Welsh pronunciation is different from English. See if you can use this and the tips in the Chapter Ten activity to pronounce the tricky names from the list of the Thirteen Treasures of Britain.

ae, ai, au – pronounced 'igh', as in 'high'.
aw – pronounced 'ow', as in 'cow'.
dd – pronounced 'th', as in 'breathe'.
f – pronounced 'v' as in 'of'.
ff – pronounced 'f' as in 'off'.
rh – pronounced 'hr' with the 'h' sound before the 'r'.

See the description for this activity on the Tales of Truth and Treasure website (truthandtreasure.com) fpr a video reading of a list of the Thirteen Treasures of Britain with authentic Welsh pronunciation.

Chapter Fifteen

Just before the intruder arrives, Meghan is devising an alternative game of football called 'gameball'. The game of football we know today has evolved over hundreds of years from medieval games where two teams would try to propel a ball to opposite ends of a playing area. Beyond that, the rules (if there were any) have been lost and probably varied a lot anyway. Rugby, Gaelic football, Australian rules football, Canadian football and American football, as well as dozens of others, share this same heritage.

See if you and your friends can come up with a version of gameball that works for you. You can use your hands, but the ball should mostly be moved by kicking, and each team needs to get it to an area at the opposite end of a playing area to score. Apart from that, it's up to you. For example, you could have two balls or an endzone for scoring instead of goals.

Chapter Sixteen

Get hold of a map of Britain (a plain printout you can draw on would be ideal) and see if you can follow the history lesson Mr and Mrs Trevelyan give Tia.

Add a compass showing North, South East and West. Mrs Trevelyan describes how the Saxons settled in and spread across the country. Draw some arrows approaching from the right-hand side of the map to show this, along with advancing soldiers bearing swords, helmets and shields.

Tia learns that, after a lot of battles and many years, the Saxons had spread across the majority of the UK. However, Cornwall, Scotland and Wales remained very Celtic. You could shade the Anglo-Saxon areas red and the Celtic areas yellow, as it looked at the end of this period, but remember that there was probably a lot of Celtic heritage mixed in with the Anglo-Saxon England.

Some place names show the long-lasting influence of Anglo-Saxon settlement in the East and South of England. For example, Essex, Middlesex and Sussex were the lands of the East Saxons, Middle Saxons and South Saxons, respectively, while Norfolk and Suffolk are the north and south parts of East Anglia, the realm of the Angles.

Chapter Seventeen

The children are doing some research into medieval hobbies in this chapter. Games and toys back then were very different, and some probably sound more interesting to you than others.

Choose one of the games the children mention to research and use a computer to produce a short PowerPoint presentation. Can you create three or four slides with effective images, clear headings and relevant information written in your own words? You could even add some medieval music or a video clip to your presentation.

Chapter Eighteen

Tia and Pasco research a game called Brandubh, which was played on a seven-by-seven board, but they aren't sure of the exact rules. Make your own gameboard (weave strips of two different colours of paper together to make a chequered board) and pieces (use small painted stones, shells or little toys) or adapt a chess set, as Tia and Pasco did. Play around with different rules about how the pieces are set up, how they can move (one square at a time or as far as they want in a straight line) and how they are captured. Decide which rules you like best.

Chapter Nineteen

In this chapter, the girls are given a replica of the figurine they unearthed. How easy is it to create a new version of something using different materials? Try making a model of a favourite object from clay. For more of a challenge, try creating a mould out of the clay, which you can then fill up with plaster of Paris.

Chapter Twenty

What is Bonfire Night all about? What is Diwali about? Although the two festivals mark very different occasions, there are similarities in the way they are celebrated.

Many festivals are traditionally celebrated across the northern hemisphere in October and November for which light is a central theme. Why do you think this might be?

Both Bonfire Night and Diwali use fireworks as part of their festivities, and you can make your own upside-down fireworks in a jar or glass. Fill your vessel three-quarters full with warm water. Add about three tablespoons of vegetable oil. Does the oil mix with the water or stay separate? Can you explain why? Mix it with a fork to break the oil into smaller globules, then add a few drops of food colouring. What happens to the food colouring when it hits the oil? What happens as it passes through the oil and meets the water? Can you explain what is happening and why?

Chapter Twenty-one

At this point in the book, Tia describes feelings of fear and anxiety, but also feelings of being safe, loved and brave. Can you compose some music to reflect these emotions?

Which instruments will you choose to reflect fear, threat and danger? Melodic or percussive instruments? Will they be played loudly or softly? Quickly or slowly? Now do the same for the positive emotions she feels by the end of the chapter: the love, warmth and safety she feels in her home and with her family. Again, choose the instruments, tempo and dynamics carefully. You may not have many purpose-built instruments to hand, but percussive instruments can be improvised from just about anything, and you can also use your voice. Play your pieces one after the other and see if listeners can guess which piece of music corresponds with which emotion.

Chapter Twenty-two

Nana Ollie shares photos of items her team discovered in the wreckage of a slave ship in the Caribbean. The slave trade involved kidnapping, imprisoning and transporting people across the ocean, shackled and in filthy confined spaces. Each slave was typically given a space of about 160 x 130cm. Mark out this space on the floor with masking tape or string, then lie down in it (no cushions allowed).

Listen to some sombre music like Barber's 'Adagio for Strings' as you lie in your space, and imagine being tossed about on the ocean for weeks on end. Remember that you would have been forcibly removed from a home you would never see again, on a voyage towards an unknown future in which you would have absolutely no power. Can you stay in your space for the whole piece of music? You will only have spent a few minutes in a space that an adult would have had to spend weeks in.

Try to express some of the feelings those people might have experienced, using words, art or whatever method you like.

Chapter Twenty-three

Ms Morgan told Mr Teague that she longs for children to "undertake a greater quest of exploration and discovery; that they'll explore their own identity and discover who they truly are".

Can you think of any experiences you've had that have helped you understand yourself better? It could be something you did for the first time and discovered you were really good at, or a hard experience you have come through. We are all very different and the world would be such a boring place if everyone was the same. Feel proud of who you are and know that this is a lifelong discovery: exploring YOU!

Chapter Twenty-four

We have now been introduced to all the key characters in the story. Chat to a friend, family member or teacher about how you picture one or more characters. Try to specifically describe the way you think they look, for example skin colour, eye colour and hair. How many did you picture as being black, Asian or minority ethnic (BAME)?

I had a clear idea in my own mind as to what each character would look like, but decided to write in a way that left their ethnicity open to the reader's interpretation, then ask them to consider why they pictured each character as they did.

Below is an explanation of how I imagine some of the characters ethnically. I did not explicitly describe them in this way, but you won't find anything in the story that contradicts these imaginings:

Tia is of white British origin.

Meghan is mixed race with a black British birth father and a white British birth mother.

Pasco is white British.

Gwen Trevelyan is mixed race with a white British father (**Grandpa Locryn**) and a white Polish mother (deceased).

Tom Trevelyan is mixed race with white British father (deceased) and black Caribbean mother (**Nana Ollie**).
Ms Morgan is black Nigerian.
Mr Teague is white Irish.
Bran is black British of Caribbean descent.

It doesn't mean you're a racist if you imagined any of these characters differently, and you don't have to change your image of them, but I would like you to think about why you pictured them the way you did.

Unfortunately, most of us live in a society that is tainted by racism to some extent, and that may mean that we subconsciously make assumptions about race for no good reason. But if we live our lives in a way that is mindful of this, perhaps things will be different in the future.

Chapter Twenty-five

People use imaginary lines to help locate where a place is in the world. Lines of latitude run parallel to the equator and tell us how far north or south a place is, while lines of longitude run between the north and south poles and tell us how far east or west it is. We record latitude and longitude in degrees, with 0 being the equator, the north pole being 90 degrees north and the south pole being 90 degrees south. 0 degrees longitude runs through Greenwich in London, and we label anything to the east 'degrees east' and to the west 'degrees west'.

The longitude and latitude co-ordinates Tia and Pasco find (53°58'56"N 0°30'27"W) are written in degrees, minutes (signified by ') and seconds (signified by "), which is the old-fashioned way of recording the co-ordinates. There are sixty minutes in one degree and sixty seconds in one minute.

Can you work out how many seconds there are in one degree? How many in thirty minutes and twenty-seven seconds? How many seconds in fifty-three degrees, fifty-eight minutes and fifty-six seconds?

Chapter Twenty-Six

Lots of the action in this chapter takes place around a church font. See what you can find out about the Christian practice of christening and how the font fits into it. What are the similarities and differences between this and adult baptism, both in practical terms and in symbolism?

Imagine a child you know was being christened. Which symbols would you use to design a card for them?

Chapter Twenty-Seven

In this chapter, Tia and Pasco are underground, walking around in the dark. This is frightening and exhilarating at the same time, and is an experience you can (almost) replicate yourself.

Head to an open space with a friend or adult, taking along some string or rope and something you can use as a blindfold. Use a local park, field or woodland where you can create an outdoor route with string or rope tied between trees to turn left, right, down slopes, up hills or behind buildings. The route must have a clear start and finish.

Wearing a blindfold, take it in turns to go around the course from start to finish, holding tight to the string with one hand. You could even go round together. How many times did you fall before you reached the finish line? This is a great activity for building trust and confidence in each other.

Chapter Twenty-Eight

At this point in the story, our heroes are terrified about the bridges collapsing around them. Working as part of a team, can you design your own bridge to span the distance between two chairs placed a metre apart, using whatever materials you have at your disposal?

Remember, the longer and heavier the bridge, and the more weight it carries, the greater risk it has of collapsing. See if you can design a bridge that will support the weight of this book, then a pile of books. Don't be afraid to stop and redesign if you need to.

Chapter Twenty-nine

The children face the test of worthiness in this chapter. Each of us is worthy of being loved, accepted, helped and happy, and of experiencing success, but sometimes we struggle to see it in ourselves. Write a note or email to a friend to remind them why you think they are such a great friend. Remind them that it is who they are that makes them special, not what they give you or do for you. It might just make their day!

Chapter Thirty

I love the idea of the magic pot in this chapter. What foods would you find in the pot of Rhygenydd if you could have anything in the world for dinner? Design a menu for your ideal three-course dinner (a starter, main course and dessert). Can you shop for ingredients, then cook and serve it to your family?

Chapter Thirty-one

Let's look at the characteristics of Mr Silverman, the story's villain. How many of the following would you attribute to him: brave, strong, clever, selfish, proud, powerful? Are there any I have missed? How about Tia? Do any of these attributes match her character? Are any missing?

On a piece of A3 paper, draw around two plates, side by side with an overlap at the centre. Arrange these characteristics in a Venn diagram with Tia on one side and Mr Silverman on the other to show any ways they are similar in the overlapping area. You could do this for any two characters (or even three, but it can get a bit tricky if you attempt more than three) from the book.

Chapter Thirty-two

Meghan describes their adventure as a treasure hunt. Can you make a treasure hunt for a friend with tests and challenges? You will need a pencil and around eight slips of paper.

Write your first positional clue, for example 'look somewhere very cold' for the freezer (or perhaps yours will be much more cryptic!) and keep hold of it. Then hide your next slip of paper in the freezer with a challenge on. It might say 'sing a nursery rhyme' or 'do ten star jumps'. On the back it must have the next positional clue, for example 'look where you wash and relax' for the bath, with the next challenge.

Create six more positional clues with challenges on the back. Hide them carefully and start a friend off with the first clue. Don't forget your 'treasure' for the end. It's always a good idea to try it out yourself first to make sure you've got the order right!

Chapter Thirty-three

This is a chapter of questions, answers and more questions. Perhaps the story has raised some questions for you. If so, I would love to hear them. Ask a parent, teacher or other adult to contact me via social media (links on the website: truthandtreasure.com) and I will do my best to reply!

Chapter Thirty-four

Activity one: Can you write a short adventure story in which a character discovers an item that initially appears ordinary but turns out to have magical properties? On your next visit to a museum, choose an artefact and concoct a story that fits with its known history. Add as much magic as you like.

Spend some time thinking about this item and its power before you plan your story. Aim for five paragraphs using a simple structure, such as 'First, Then, Next, After, Finally'. Think about ways of improving your writing like authors do by improving the vocabulary, punctuation and flow.

Activity two: In this final chapter we discover that Tia's name is an anagram. That means the letters of her name can be rearranged to create a new word or phrase. Your final challenge is to try this with the letters from your own name. Your full name might give you more options. Can you create a word or phrase using all the letters from your name? If not, can you create a list of words your name contains? You could also try it with the names of friends, family members, famous people or just about any words really. You might be surprised how many secret messages there are out there just waiting to be unscrambled…

Acknowledgements

Thank you to all those who have read and offered insights into the various drafts of Tia's journey, especially Anna Griffin, Scott Thomson and Linden Hansen.

Thank you to everyone at Emira Press for believing in this tale, and for all the incredible work you've put into getting it out there. Particular thanks to Clair Lansley for the beautiful design work.

Thank you, Mum and Dad, for giving me a secure and loving childhood that enabled me to dream, imagine and believe.

Thank you, Rach, Lily, Tom and Benji, for all the adventures, without which I would not have been able to write the ones contained in these pages.

Thank you, Jesus, for helping me believe in the beauty and to bear the brokenness of life.

About the author

James Haddell has always loved stories and adventure. He spent most of his childhood reading and daydreaming in Kent, then went to university in Durham to study maths and economics. Then four months spent volunteering for a Thai charity for children with disabilities in Bangkok after university changed everything.

James trained as a primary school teacher, working in various schools in London before getting married and moving back to Thailand for seven years, where he began writing the Tales of Truth and Treasure series. After adopting two children, he returned to the UK and worked in a number of primary school and nursery settings as a teacher and as a special educational needs and disability co-ordinator.

James currently lives in Somerset with his wife and three children, where he spends his time writing, teaching, and being a husband and dad… though he still finds time to do a little reading and daydreaming now and then.